Lynn Raye Harris

THE PRINCE'S
ROYAL CONCUBINE

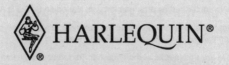

HARLEQUIN®

TORONTO • NEW YORK • LONDON
AMSTERDAM • PARIS • SYDNEY • HAMBURG
STOCKHOLM • ATHENS • TOKYO • MILAN • MADRID
PRAGUE • WARSAW • BUDAPEST • AUCKLAND

Recycling programs
for this product may
not exist in your area.

ISBN-13: 978-0-373-12925-6

THE PRINCE'S ROYAL CONCUBINE

First North American Publication 2010.

THE PRINCE'S
ROYAL CONCUBINE

To all the editors at Harlequin Mills & Boon
for holding a competition to find new writers
and for choosing me as their winner. I am truly
honored by your faith in me, and thankful for
the opportunity you have given me. But most
especially to my editor, Sally Williamson, who
pushes me to be the best I can be and encourages
me to stretch my wings with each book.

CHAPTER ONE

PRINCE CRISTIANO DI SAVARÉ slipped the last stud into his tuxedo shirt and straightened the points of his collar as he gazed at his reflection. The yacht rocked gently beneath his feet, but that was the only indication he was on board a ship and not in a luxury hotel room. He'd flown over two thousand miles to be here tonight and, though he wasn't tired, the expression on his face was grim. So grim that lines bracketed his mouth, furrowed his forehead, and made him look older than his thirty-one years.

He would have to work on that before he hunted his quarry. Though his task tonight gave him no joy, it had to be done. He forced a smile, studied it. Yes, that would work.

Women always melted when he turned on the charm.

He shrugged into his jacket and whisked a spot of lint away with a flick of his fingers. What would Julianne think if she saw him now? He'd give anything for another glimpse of her, for the little pout on her face whenever she concentrated— as she surely would while she straightened his tie and implored him not to look so serious.

Cristiano turned away from the mirror, unwilling to see the expression he now wore at the thought of his dead wife. He'd been married for so short a time—and so long ago now that he sometimes couldn't remember the exact shade of Julianne's hair or the way her laugh sounded. Was that normal?

He knew it was, and yet it both angered and saddened him. She'd paid the ultimate price for marrying him. He would never forgive himself for allowing her to die when he could have prevented it. *Should* have prevented it.

It was four and a half years since he'd let her climb onto a helicopter destined for the volatile border between Monterosso and Monteverde. In spite of the unease churning in his gut, he'd let her go without him.

Julianne had been a medical student, and she'd insisted on accompanying him on an aid mission. When he had to cancel at the last moment, he should have ordered her to stay behind with him.

But she'd convinced him that the new Crown Princess should work toward peace with Monteverde. As an American, she'd felt safe enough visiting both countries. She'd been certain she could make a difference.

And he'd let her certainty convince him.

Cristiano closed his eyes. The news that a Monteverdian bomb had ended Julianne's life, and the lives of three aid workers with her, triggered the kind of rage and despair he'd never experienced before or since.

It was his fault. She would have lived if he'd refused to let her go. Would have lived if he'd never married her. Why had he done so? He'd asked himself that question many times since.

He didn't believe in lightning bolts and love at first sight, but he'd been drawn to her. The attraction between them had been strong, and he'd been certain marrying her was the right decision.

Except that it hadn't been. Not for her.

The truth was that he'd done it for selfish reasons. He'd

needed to marry, and he'd refused to allow his father to dictate who his bride would be. Instead, he'd chosen a bold, beautiful girl he barely knew simply because the sex was great and he liked her very much. He'd swept her off her feet, promised her the world.

And she'd believed him. Far better if she hadn't.

Basta!

He dropped a mental shield into place, slicing off his thoughts. He would be unfit for mingling with Raúl Vega's guests if he did not do so. Those dark days were over. He'd found a purpose in their aftermath, and he would not rest until it was done.

Monteverde.

The princess. The reason he was here.

"It is a beautiful night, is it not?"

Princess Antonella Romanelli spun from her cabin door to find a man leaning against the railing, watching her. Faintly, the ocean lapped the yacht's sides, someone laughed on another ship anchored not too far away, and the smell of jasmine hung in the air.

But her gaze was locked on the dark form of the man. His tuxedo blended into the night, making him nothing more than a silhouette against the backdrop of Canta Paradiso's city lights. Then he stepped forward and the light from the deck illuminated his face.

She recognized him instantly, though they'd never met. That handsome countenance—the jet-dark hair, the sharp cheekbones, the sensual lips—belonged to only one man in the whole world. The absolute last man she should be talking to at this moment.

Or ever.

Antonella drew in a sharp breath, fighting for that famous

detachment for which she was renowned. Dear God, why was he here? What did he want? Did he know how desperate she was?

Of course not—don't be silly!

"Cat got your tongue, I see."

Antonella swallowed, willed her thrumming heart to beat normally. He was more beautiful in person than in the photos she'd seen. And more dangerous. Tension rolled from him, enveloping her in his dark presence. *His unexpected presence.* Warning bells clanged in her mind. "Not at all. You merely surprised me."

His gaze raked over her slowly, leaving her skin prickling in its wake. "We have not been introduced," he said smoothly, his voice as rich and alluring as dark chocolate. "I am Cristiano di Savaré."

"I know who you are," Antonella said—and then cursed herself for saying it so quickly. As if words were weapons and she could use them to push him away.

"Yes, I imagine you do."

He made it sound like an insult. Antonella drew herself up with all the dignity and hauteur a princess could manage. "And why wouldn't I recognize the name of the Crown Prince of Monterosso?"

Her country's bitterest rival. Though the history between the three sister-nations—Monteverde, Montebianco, and Monterosso—was tangled, it was only Monteverde and Monterosso that remained at war to this day. Antonella thought of the Monteverdian soldiers stationed on the volatile border tonight, of the razor wire fences, the landmines and tanks, and a pang of dark emotion ricocheted through her.

They were there for her, for everyone in Monteverde. They kept her nation safe from invasion. She could not fail them—or the rest of her people—in her mission here. *Would* not. Her nation would not disappear off the face of this earth simply because her father was a tyrannical brute who'd bankrupted his country and driven it to the very edge of oblivion.

"I would not expect it otherwise, *Principessa,*" he said with cool certainty.

Arrogant man. She lifted her chin. *Never let them see your fear, Ella,* her brother always said. "What are you doing here?"

His grin was not what she expected, a flash of impossibly white teeth in the gloom. And about as friendly as a lion's feral growl. The hair on the back of her neck stood up.

"The same as you, I imagine. Raúl Vega is a very wealthy man, *si*? He could bring many jobs to a country fortunate enough to win his business."

Antonella's blood froze. *She* needed Raúl Vega, not this…this arrogant, too-handsome man who already had all the advantages of his power and position. Monterosso was wealthy beyond compare; Monteverde *needed* Vega Steel to survive. It was life or death for her people. Since her father had been deposed, her brother had been holding the country together through sheer force of will. But it wouldn't last much longer. They needed foreign investment, needed someone with the clout of Vega to come in and show other investors through example that the country was still a good bet.

The astronomical loans her father had taken out were coming due, and they had no money to pay them. Extensions were out of the question. Though Dante and the government had acted in the nation's best interest when they'd deposed her father, creditor nations had viewed the events with trepidation and suspicion. To them, requests for loan extensions would mean Monteverde was seeking ways to have the loans declared void.

A commitment from Vega Steel would change that.

If Cristiano di Savaré knew how close they were to the brink of collapse—

No. He couldn't know. No one could. Not yet, though her country couldn't hide it for much longer. Soon the world would know. And Monteverde would cease to exist. The thought dripped courage into her veins, each dose stronger than the last until she was brimming with it.

"I am surprised Monterosso cares about Vega Steel," she said coolly. "And my interest in Signor Vega has nothing to do with business."

Cristiano smirked, but it was too late to take back the words. She'd meant to deflect him, but she'd opened herself up to ridicule instead. *Careless.*

"Ah, yes, I have heard about this. About you."

Antonella pulled her silk shawl closer over the pale cream designer gown she wore. He made her feel cheap—small and dirty and insignificant—without saying one word of what he truly meant. He didn't need to; the implication was clear.

"If you are finished, Your Highness?" she said frostily. "I believe I am expected at dinner."

He moved closer, so nearly into her personal space that it must be intentional. He was tall and broad, and it took everything she had not to shrink from him. She'd spent years cowering before her father when he was in a rage; when he'd been arrested six months ago, she'd promised herself she would not cower before a man ever again.

She stood rigid, waiting. Trembling, and hating herself for the weakness.

"Allow me to escort you, *Principessa*, for I am headed in the same direction."

He was so close, so real. So intimidating. "I can find my own way."

"Of course." His smile didn't reach his eyes.

Beneath his studied demeanor, she sensed hostility. Darkness. Emptiness.

He continued, "But if you refuse, I might think you afraid of me."

Antonella swallowed, forced her throat to work. *Too close to the mark.* "Why on earth would I be afraid of you?"

"Precisely." He held out his arm, daring her to accept.

She hesitated. But there was no way out and she would not run like a frightened child. It was a betrayal of Monteverde to be seen with him—and yet this was the Caribbean; Monteverde was thousands of miles away. No one would ever know.

"Very well." She laid her hand on his arm—and nearly jerked away at the sizzle skimming through her. Touching Cristiano was like touching lightning. She thought he flinched, but she couldn't be sure.

Was that brimstone she smelled? It wouldn't surprise her—he was the devil incarnate so far as she was concerned.

The enemy.

But, no, it was simply her imagination. He smelled like a sea-swept night, fresh and clean with a hint of spice. When his hand settled over hers, she had to force down a sense of panic. She felt trapped, and yet his grip was light. Impersonal perhaps. It was the touch of a man schooled in protocol, a man escorting a woman to an event.

It was nothing.

And yet—

Yet her heart tripped as if it were on a downhill plunge. There was something about him, something dark and danger-ous and altogether different from the type of men she usually met.

"You have been in the Caribbean long?" he asked as they strolled along the outer deck.

"A few days," she replied absently, wondering how to make him pick up the pace. At this rate, it would take several minutes to reach the grand ballroom. Several minutes in which she would be alone in his company. "But I haven't seen much of the island yet."

"No, I don't imagine you would."

Antonella ground to a halt at his tone. *Smug, superior.* "What is that supposed to mean?"

He turned toward her, his eyes slipping down her body, back up again. Evaluating her. Judging her. Oddly enough, she found herself wanting to know what color they were. Blue? Grey like her own? She couldn't tell in the yellowish light from the deck lamps. But they left her shivering and achy all at once.

"It means, *Principessa*, that when you spend much of your time on your back, you can hardly expect to do much sightseeing."

She couldn't stifle a gasp. "How dare you pretend to know me—"

"Who does *not* know you, Antonella Romanelli? In the past six months, you have certainly made yourself known. You parade around Europe dressed in the latest fashions, attending all the *best* parties, and sleeping with whoever catches your fancy at the moment. Like Vega."

If he'd notched an arrow and aimed it straight at her heart, it could have hurt no worse.

What could she possibly say to defend herself? Why did she even want to?

Antonella spun away, but Cristiano caught her wrist and prevented her from escaping. His grip was harder than any she'd imagined. Her heart raced so hard she was afraid she'd grow light-headed. Her father was a strong man. A man with a hair-trigger temper and a quick fist when angered. She'd borne the brunt of that fist more times than she cared to remember.

"Let me go," she bit out, her skin prickling with icy fear.

"Your brother should control you better," he said—but his grip loosened and she jerked free, rubbing her wrist though he had not hurt her.

Anger slid into place, crowded out the fear. "Who do you think you are? Just because you're the heir to the Monterossan throne does not make you special to *me*. And my life is none of your business." Her laugh was bitter. "I know what you think of me, of my people. But know this—you have not beaten us in over one thousand years and you will not do so now."

"Bravo," he said, eyes glittering dangerously. "Very passionate. One wonders how passionate you might be in other circumstances."

"You will have to continue to wonder, *Your Highness*. Because I would throw myself over the side of this yacht before ever entertaining a man such as you in my bed."

Not that she'd ever entertained *any* man in her bed—but he didn't know that. Regardless that she'd never found a man she trusted enough to give herself to, that she was still a virgin, all it took were a few parties, a few rumors, and a few photos to turn the truth into a lie. Most men believed her sophisticated and worldly, and the one she'd actually been brave enough to date once she'd been free of her father's iron grasp had told the lie he'd slept with her after she'd rebuffed him. Others had taken up the rallying cry until it was impossible to separate truth from rumor.

God, men made her sick. And this one was no different.

They could not see beneath the surface, which was why she primped and pampered and wore the careful exterior of a worldly princess. Her beauty was her only asset since she'd never been allowed to pursue any kind of profession.

It was also her shield. When she focused the attention on her physical appearance, she didn't need to share her secrets or fears with anyone. She could hide beneath her exterior, secure in the knowledge that no one could hurt her that way.

The sound of Cristiano's mocking laughter startled her back to the moment. She realized too late that she'd just done the unthinkable. She'd challenged a man with a legendary reputation for bedding women. A man about whom women spoke in tones of rapture and awe. She might not have anything to do with the Monterossans, but she'd heard the gossip about their Crown Prince.

He'd been married once, but his wife was dead. Since then, no woman had held his attention for longer than a few weeks, a couple of months at most. He was a serial dater and a heartbreaker. A smooth operator, as her friend Lily, the Crown Princess of Montebianco, would have said.

"Perhaps nothing so desperate as that," he said, closing the distance between them. Antonella took a step backward, coming into contact with the solid wall of the yacht. Cristiano put a hand on either side of her head, trapping her. He leaned closer without touching her. "Should we test this vow of yours with a kiss?"

"You can't be serious," she gasped.

He loomed over her. Dark. Intense. "Why not?"

"You're Monterossan!"

He laughed again, but there was no humor in it. It confused her—or maybe it was simply his overwhelming nearness bewildering her senses.

His head dipped toward her. "Indeed. But you are a woman, and I'm a man. The night is warm, lush, perfect for passion…"

For a moment, she was paralyzed. Any second his mouth would claim hers, any second she would feel the hot press of his lips, any second her soul would be in danger—because something about him sent her pulse skyrocketing. Her nipples tightened, her skin itched, and the deep, secret recesses of her body felt as if they were softening, melting—

At the last possible moment, when his lips were a hair's breadth away, when his hot breath mingled with hers, she found her strength and ducked beneath an imprisoning arm. He caught himself, shoving away from the side of the yacht.

Swore.

"Very good, Antonella. But then you are quite practiced at this game, aren't you?"

Antonella held herself rigid. Why did her name sound so exotic when he said it? "You're despicable. You seek to take what is not yours, and you resort to force to get it. Exactly what I would expect from a Monterossan."

If she thought to anger him, she was disappointed. He merely smiled that wolfish smile of his. The ice in it made her shudder.

"Excuses, excuses, *Principessa*. That is what your country is good at, *si*? Because you are not as successful or as wealthy as us, you blame us for your ills. And you take innocent lives to justify your hostility."

"I'm not listening to this," she said, turning away from him. She had no time to engage in an argument with him. Nor would it do any good. She would simply be upset, and she couldn't afford the distraction right now.

"Yes, run away to your steel magnate. But let us see what he values most—his mistress or his bank account."

Antonella whirled. He'd dropped all pretense of friendliness; his voice dripped menace. "What do you mean by that?"

Cristiano stalked closer and once again she found herself trapped. Not physically this time, but it felt the same as if he'd grabbed her and refused to let her move. Her feet may as well have been glued to the teak decking.

"It means, *bellissima Principessa,* that I too have a proposition for Vega." His gaze slid over her, and again she felt as if she'd stood too close to a lightning strike. "I am betting that my money trumps your…shall we say…*obvious* charms."

"How dare you—"

"I believe you have said this already, yes? It grows tiring."

Antonella trembled with fury. The man was impossible, aggravating—and having the most incredible effect on her senses. Surely it was anger that made her flush hot and cold, that made her skin tingle. He was threatening to ruin all her hard work, to turn Vega away before she'd managed to hook him. She *had* to get those steel mills for Monteverde. *Had to.*

And in order to do it, she needed to focus. Needed to will her heightened senses to calm. Needed to cloak herself in her ice princess mantle. No matter how this man made her feel, no matter how hot and achy and angry she was, she *had* to play this right.

Antonella dug down deep, found what she was searching for. By degrees, she felt her body loosening from its rigid stance. Felt confidence and calm wash over her. She would not let him intimidate her.

"Perhaps we have started on the wrong foot," she purred. She needed to misdirect him, befuddle him. To do that, she would play the part he'd given her, make him believe there was indeed a chance of sex. It would buy her a little bit of time, at least. She could hold out the promise of a night together, keep him guessing while she worked hard to reel in Vega Steel before he could snatch victory from her.

In spite of her inexperience, it wasn't difficult to act the part. At times like this, she disappeared deep within herself, separated her inner being from the shell and watched everything from outside the scene. It was the only way she could cope—by pretending to be someone else. It was a skill she'd honed over years of living with an abusive father.

Cristiano stood his ground as she reached for him, as her fingertips stroked along his freshly shaven jaw, over the fullness of his hard mouth, his chin.

His eyes were impossible to read. And then something kindled in their depths, something that both frightened her and compelled her. Perhaps she was going too far, making a mistake…

"You play with fire, *Principessa*," he growled.

She worked hard to ignore the warning bells in her head as she slipped her hand around to the back of his neck, into the soft hair at his nape, bringing herself closer as she did so. Could she really do this?

She could, and she would. Let him see what a Monteverdian was made of. He would not intimidate her. He would not win.

Slowly, she pulled his head down. So slowly. He didn't try to move away, simply followed her bidding. She didn't kid herself she was in control. He was interested, like a cat was interested in a mouse.

But, for now, he let her guide him. And that was all she needed.

When he was only inches away, she stroked her fingers down his jaw again. Over that gorgeous mouth because she couldn't help herself. She couldn't play it too easy, of course, because he would see right through her. But if she got him worked up a bit, made him think about how to storm her defenses, she might buy enough time to get Raúl to commit to Monteverde.

"Know this," she said softly, her voice as sultry as she could make it. "Know that you have been this close to paradise…" She lifted herself onto her tiptoes, leaned in so close that her lips could have ghosted over his with little effort. "…this close, Cristiano," she said, using his name for the first time. "And no further."

Then she took a step back, intending to leave him standing there, puzzling over what had just happened.

A split second later, Cristiano caught her waist in two large hands, yanked her against the full length of his hard body. The wild thought that she should have run while she'd had the chance flashed into her mind. Instead, she'd pushed the thorn deeper into the lion's paw when she should have given him a wide berth.

Cristiano's mouth crushed down on hers with devastating precision. The kiss was masterful, dominating, unlike any she'd ever experienced before. Antonella's head tilted back as he bracketed her face between two broad hands. He slanted his mouth over hers, forced a response. When she opened her lips—to protest? To bite him? To do what?—his tongue slipped inside and tangled with her own.

Heat flooded her like melting wax, dripped into her limbs, made her languid and pliable when she should be anything but. He'd caught her by surprise and she couldn't seem to separate herself from the act. It wasn't the first time she'd been kissed—but it was the first time she'd felt on the verge of losing herself in a kiss.

She wanted to dissolve into him, wanted to see where this hot achy feeling would take her if she let it. It was marvelous, extraordinary—

Reality trickled through her as his hands slipped down her back, over her hips, pulled her against his body. His hard, tense body.

Oh, my, was that—?

No. She couldn't do this. He was the *enemy*, for God's sake! She fought against nature, against him, against *herself* to claw her way back to the surface.

And though it was a cheap thing to do, she bit down on his questing tongue just enough to make him withdraw. It was that or allow him to so completely dominate her senses that she lost the power of her convictions.

He swore. And then he laughed. Actually *laughed*. "You need a spanking, *cara*. I'll be sure to remedy that when we are naked together."

Antonella managed to jerk free from his grip. She was off-balance, her heart pounding and her blood simmering, and she wanted nothing more than to escape. But she had to stand firm.

She jerked her shawl back into place. "If this is how you usually set about your seductions, it's a wonder you have any success at all."

His eyes burned into her. "When I want something, I get it. Always."

Against her will, a hot little flame smoldered deep inside. She had to get away, far away. "I can't say it's been a pleasure meeting you, but if you will excuse me, my *lover* is waiting. Ciao."

"For now, *Principessa*," he said. "But I have a feeling you will take a new lover quite soon."

She'd made a mistake thinking she could manage him. A huge mistake. And yet she desperately wanted to wipe the smirk from his face. She gave him her best ice princess glare. "Yes, well, that man will *not* be you."

"Never make promises you cannot keep. The first lesson of statecraft."

"This isn't a negotiation between nations."

"Isn't it?"

When she couldn't think of a rejoinder, she pivoted and hurried to the dining room. Raúl stood on the opposite side of the room, speaking with a short, bald man. He looked up when he saw her, smiled. She smiled back. He was a handsome man, tall and rather good-looking in his custom tuxedo.

But he did not make her blood hum. Not the way Cristiano seemed to do. Angrily, she shoved away thoughts of the prince and crossed to Raúl's side, letting him kiss her on both cheeks in greeting.

"There you are, Antonella. I was about to send a search party."

Antonella laughed. Was she the only one who thought the sound brittle, false? Other guests clustered together, talking and sipping cocktails. A few watched her from beneath lowered lids. One man stared openly.

"I'm afraid I must always be fashionably late, darling," she said.

Raúl swiped a champagne glass from a passing tray and handed it to her. She murmured her thanks before lifting it to her lips. Cristiano di Savaré walked in at the moment she sipped.

Her pulse jumped and she swallowed too much of the bubbly liquid, coughing as it seared a path down her throat.

Raúl failed to notice as he murmured, "Excuse me a moment, my dear," and strode over to Cristiano.

Oh, God. She had to keep them apart. She had to convince Raúl to invest in Monteverde *tonight*. There was no time to lose. She wasn't about to let that arrogant, rude bastard derail her plans.

Just as she got the coughing under control and started toward the two men, someone bumped her elbow.

Antonella held her glass out in time to prevent a spill. An elderly woman in a garish tropical-print muumuu gasped, her hand over her heart as if she were having an attack. "Please excuse me, Your Highness! Oh, how clumsy of me!"

"No, no, it is fine," Antonella said, her voice a little rough from the coughing. "I didn't spill a drop."

But the woman was unconvinced and insisted on a thorough inspection. Then it took several more minutes for Antonella to disentangle from the ensuing conversation. Once the poor lady seemed soothed, Antonella moved away with a murmured apology and went looking for Raúl.

It didn't take her long to realize the frightening truth, however.

Raúl had left the room. And so had the Crown Prince of Monterosso.

CHAPTER TWO

SHE stood for everything he despised.

Cristiano sat at the polished mahogany table, directly across from Antonella Romanelli, and watched as she directed all her attention on Raúl Vega. Vega basked in her lovely glow like a man showing off a prized possession.

And why not?

She wore an ivory silk gown that clung to her body like a sleeve and displayed her breasts to perfection. With her sooty fall of hair, generous cleavage, and sharp sense of self-awareness, Princess Antonella was the kind of woman who lit up a room simply by entering it. He'd seen photos of her, but nothing had actually prepared him for the impact of her physical beauty. She was, in a word, stunning.

She had a voice that reminded him of a hidden spring, sweet and pure until she poured on the honey, and a sensual way of moving that made a man's mind turn to more elemental matters. When she'd turned to him outside her cabin door, he'd felt as if a weight had settled on his chest and wouldn't lift. He'd come prepared for battle, certain he was more than ready for it, and been felled by a lightning strike to his gut.

Dio.

He had to remember that without the Romanellis, peace

would have come to Monterosso and Monteverde many years ago. Countless people would have lived instead of dying senseless, bloody deaths.

Paolo Romanelli had been an egomaniacal despot. His son, Dante, was certainly no better. He'd deposed his own father, after all. What kind of son did that? What kind of daughter flitted around the world, taking and discarding lovers, seemingly indifferent to her family's excesses?

He'd counted on that indifference to help him gain what he wanted. Antonella was a woman of expensive tastes and a dwindling bank account. He had the means to keep her in designer gowns and expensive spa treatments, yet he'd nearly blown the whole game with his visceral reaction to her on deck. He needed her pliable, not bristling with indignation.

Cristiano's fingers tightened on the stem of the wine glass he held. He had a chance to end it. A chance to crush Monteverde into submission once and for all. Once he gained control of their government and deposed the Romanellis, children from both nations would grow up happy and free instead of living in fear of bombs and bullets.

There was currently a ceasefire, but it was tentative. One random bomb from an extremist group, and even that fragile peace would be in jeopardy.

He intended to make it permanent, no matter the personal cost. No matter who he had to destroy.

Antonella laughed, the sound light and bubbly. So what if she was beautiful, so what if she seemed to possess a hint of vulnerability that intrigued him? Because surely it was an act. A very polished, very accomplished act. He'd known women like her before. Spoiled and shallow, nothing more than beautiful exteriors with empty souls.

Raúl bent toward her. At the last second, she expertly turned her head and his kiss landed on her cheek. Interesting.

Cristiano took a sip of wine. She thought she had Raúl wrapped up and tied with a pretty bow, but she was mistaken. Cristiano had gone to a lot of trouble to sweeten his deal. Though Raúl had yet to commit, he would not refuse Monterosso's offer. He was far too good a businessman to allow a woman, no matter how enticing, to divert him from his company's best interests.

For the first time since they'd sat at the table, Antonella's gaze landed on him. He felt the jolt to his toes, and it irritated him. He refused to look away first. A pale flush crept over her cheeks as their gazes held.

He wouldn't have thought she had it in her to be embarrassed, but perhaps sitting in the company of her current lover while contemplating another man was a bit much even for one so jaded as she.

Raúl's hand came down on Antonella's and she jumped, her head whipping around to look at him. Her flush deepened and Cristiano felt a stab of triumph. She wanted him, no matter what she'd said on the deck. It was a start in the right direction.

She looked guilty as hell as Raúl gazed at her with concern. "Are you feeling well, my dear?" Raúl said. "You look distressed."

"What? Oh—no, I'm fine. It's just a little hot. Don't you find the tropics rather hot?" she asked the gathered diners.

Several people chimed in with opinions and a discussion ensued about the balmy temperatures, the fact it was hurricane season, and whether or not—God help him—a Piña Colada was preferable to a Bahama Mama. Empty chatter that scraped across his raw nerves and made him resent her even more.

When dinner was finally over, the guests adjourned to the deck to watch the fireworks over Canta Paradiso. Antonella, he noticed, clung to Raúl as if she were afraid to let him out of her sight again.

Too late, mia bella.

"Ah, Cristiano," Raúl said as he guided Antonella over to the railing where Cristiano stood, "are you enjoying yourself in this lovely paradise?"

"*Si.* The scenery is quite…extraordinary."

Antonella dropped her gaze as his own slipped over her. Was that another blush?

Raúl failed to notice the exchange. "I still can't believe it's been five years since last we met."

Antonella blinked up at her lover. "You know the Prince?"

"We attended Harvard together," Raúl replied, breaking into a broad smile as he clapped Cristiano on the back.

"Actually, it's only been *four* years since we last met, Raúl."

"Ah, yes," Raúl said, clearing his throat. They both knew that Cristiano hadn't exactly been the best of company in the several months after Julianne's death. He'd been bitter, angry. And he'd pushed his friends and family away with equal measures of wounded contempt.

"We must not allow so much time to pass again, yes?" Cristiano said.

Raúl gave him a solemn smile. "As you say, *mi amigo.*"

Antonella's lush lower lip was fixed between her teeth. A frown drew her sculpted brows together, furrowed her forehead.

An arrow of heat shot to Cristiano's groin. All his senses had gone on high alert the moment he caught a whiff of her luscious scent. Lavender and vanilla? A hint of lemon? He'd wanted to drown in it when he'd kissed her, wanted to breathe her in for as long as he could.

The thought both angered and intrigued him. How could

he react so strongly to this woman? He had not come here with any real intention of seducing her. He'd thought his business could be concluded with a great deal of money, perhaps some flattery. An empty promise or two.

Yet his body was beginning to insist on the idea of a seduction.

It was time to close this deal and move on to the real business at hand before he became any more distracted. "Raúl, if you can spare some time now, I'd like to conclude our discussion. I'm afraid I must return to Monterosso in the morning."

Raúl nodded. "Yes, of course. If you will excuse us, my dear?" he said to Antonella.

"I must speak with you as well," she said, her voice rising. "And I'd rather do it now."

She looked fierce, like an Amazon warrior. Determined.

Raúl seemed puzzled. And perhaps a bit annoyed. Cristiano laughed inwardly. She was making it too easy for him. No man liked petulant demands from his lover, and especially not in front of witnesses. A shrewd woman would have stated her case when they were in bed together later. Her problem, not his.

"Go ahead, Raúl," Cristiano said. "I'll be here when you've finished."

He could afford to be generous. She'd just lost the game.

Antonella wanted to scream. It'd been more than an hour since Raúl and Cristiano di Savaré had disappeared for their talk. What was happening? What if Raúl decided to build his mills in Monterosso?

She'd done her best to convince him, but she didn't have a good feeling about it. What could Monteverde do for Vega Steel? They had vast deposits of raw ore, a necessary ingredient in steel, but they had little else to offer.

Except for a royal title. Yes, she'd put that on the table too when she'd sensed Raúl's reluctance to commit to her country. Why not? She'd been intended since birth to marry for Monteverde's best interests. Her father was no longer King, and she'd had two royal alliances fall through before the weddings could happen, but that didn't mean she didn't owe it to her people to do her part.

Desperate times called for desperate measures. If her choice was marriage to a man she didn't love or the annexation of her country, she'd take marriage.

No matter how angry it made her. No matter how helpless she felt, how useless. *Madonna mia*, couldn't her father have at least let her attend university instead of finishing school? She could pour tea and work a room with the best hostesses out there. And yet what good were those skills?

Raúl had taken the offer in his stride, but was it enough to convince him? In spite of his humble upbringing and his rise from poverty to great wealth, she had a feeling she'd failed miserably. If any man should have been tempted by a royal title, it should have been Raúl Vega.

If she failed, it would be yet another humiliation to add to her long list. Her first fiancé had driven a car off a cliff and her second had married another woman before the handshake had grown cold on the deal her father had made to wed her to him.

She was doomed in love, it would seem. Not that she'd ever been in love, but she'd like a chance to experience it. Like Lily, the woman her second *almost*-fiancé had married instead of her. What was it like to have a man look at you the way Nico Cavelli looked at Lily? To have a man sacrifice everything to be with you?

She would never know. It wasn't her lot in life to find love. Dante had told her she didn't need to marry for

Monteverde now that their father was no longer King, but she'd insisted it was her duty. If it benefited her country, she would do it. No matter how desperate and sad it made her. No matter how much the idea of tying herself to a man terrified her.

Not all men were like her father. Not all men would grow violent when they were angry.

Antonella shook her head to clear it. She didn't know for certain that she had failed this time. There was still a chance she'd won, that her royal title and her ore would be more enticing than anything Cristiano di Savaré had to offer.

She threw the tail of her shawl over her shoulder and continued her pacing on deck. Most of Raúl's guests had returned to shore or to their own yachts, with the exception of those who had cabins aboard. In the harbor, yachts, a cruise ship, and fishing boats lay at anchor for the night, though the sounds of laughter and music drifted across the bay.

She chewed on the edge of a fingernail, then jerked her hand away with a curse when she realized what she was doing. She hadn't chewed her nails since she was twelve and her father made her drink half a bottle of hot sauce to end the habit. It had certainly worked—she'd spent two days so sick she'd thought she would die; afterwards, she could hardly look at her fingernails without retching.

But Cristiano unsettled her in ways she couldn't quite fathom. He was Monterossan, which was a big strike against him. He was the future King of that nation, an even bigger strike. He was tall, incredibly magnetic, and arrogant beyond all imagination.

And yet, a little thrill of excitement insisted on rearing its ugly head whenever she thought about him. *Stop.* She didn't like him, and she damn sure didn't trust him.

A shiver slid over her. What if she'd failed?

"Perhaps you should drink fewer espressos so late at night, *cara.*"

Antonella whirled to find Cristiano emerging onto the deck. Her heart thumped, though not from fright. Why did he disconcert her so? "What are you talking about?"

He tipped his chin to her. "Pacing. Less caffeine would help."

Antonella closed her eyes and counted to five. He knew he irritated her. Worse, he seemed to take great pleasure in it. She must not allow him to do so any longer. She could control her reactions. *Would* control them.

"I had one espresso, *grazie*. Your concern is touching."

He came over and leaned against the rail, watching her. His eyes dipped to her chest, back up. Typical. Half the time, men talked exclusively to her breasts. She'd grown quite accustomed to it.

"You are dying to know what we talked about, aren't you?"

Antonella shrugged. "You are mistaken if you think I care. I'm not here for business."

He laughed. "So you have said. But what do they call it now, if not the oldest business in the world?"

She would not react. Would *not.* Had Raúl told him what they'd discussed, that she'd offered herself in exchange for the mills? Or was he simply baiting her?

"Is that what it's called when *you* sleep around, Cristiano?" she said very coolly, her heart throbbing with hurt and anger and the urge to deny she'd ever slept with any man. He'd never believe her, of course. Nor did he deserve an explanation.

Why did men have a double standard when it came to sex? He could bed countless women and it only added to his allure.

"Sensitive, *cara?*"

"Not at all. I simply don't like you. Or your hypocrisy."

"I'm hurt." His teeth flashed in a grin.

She wished he'd jump off the side of the yacht and leave her alone. "Where is Raúl?" she demanded.

"I'm not your social secretary, *Principessa*. If you want him, go find him." The words were said mildly, almost mockingly. And with a hint of steel beneath the velvet. "And what makes you think I'm a hypocrite? I quite like that you've had lovers. It means you know your way around a man's body. It means we will not need to waste time once we are naked."

Perhaps she'd had too much caffeine after all. Her pulse raced like a bullet fired from a gun. "I'm not sleeping with you, Cristiano."

"Don't be too sure," he said, his voice a sensual growl that scraped over her nerve endings and left her shivering.

"I know my own mind, and I know what I *don't* want. I don't want you."

Cristiano reached for her hand, slipped his fingers between hers and brought them to his mouth. She tried to pull away, but he held her firm. "And do you know your *body*, Antonella? Often, our mind and our body are at war. Did you not know that?"

Before she could formulate an answer from her scattered thoughts, he touched the tip of his tongue to the center of her palm.

Antonella sucked in a breath as rivers of sensation spilled down her spine, through her limbs, into her feminine core. Why? *Why*? Men had been trying to get her into bed for as long as she could remember and she'd yet to feel anything remotely as exciting as what she felt when Cristiano touched her.

Too bad he was the wrong man. She needed to pull her hand away forcefully, needed to put distance between them and never allow herself to be alone with him again.

But she couldn't. She was trapped, as trapped as if he'd bound her to him with iron shackles.

"Stop," she forced out, her voice little more than a tortured whisper.

"Are you quite certain?" he murmured. "Your body says otherwise."

"You don't know that."

"*Si,* I do. You are flushed…"

"It's hot."

Cristiano laughed low in his throat, kissed her fingers and settled her hand on his shoulder before he tugged her closer. His broad fingers splayed over her hip. "And it's about to get hotter. Why deny this attraction, hmm? We will be good together."

"I—"

A shadow passed over them and then a voice said, "I beg your pardon."

Antonella jerked out of Cristiano's grip just in time to see Raúl turn around and slip back inside. Oh, God! Furious tears pressed against the back of her eyes but she refused to let them fall. She would have to go after him, would have to try and repair the damage. She'd just offered to marry him, for God's sake. What would he think of her now?

She *could* repair the damage. Surely she could. *She had to.* For Monteverde's future.

But not before she turned and gave the arrogant man who'd caused her so much trouble in such a short time a piece of her mind.

"You did that on purpose!" She should have listened to the voice telling her to get away from him. Because she hadn't, because she'd been riveted by his handsome face and sizzling touch, she'd risked the future of her entire nation. And for what? A kiss? A kiss from a man she despised?

He wasn't insane; *she was.*

"What makes you think so, *Principessa?*" he asked coolly, his expression both smug and devilish at once.

Antonella's hands clenched into impotent fists as her heartbeat thundered in her ears. She was a fool, a hopeless fool, still looking for some spark of feeling with a man. And he was the enemy, plain and simple. He hadn't forgotten it for one moment, even if she had.

"Because you're selfish, that's why. You don't care who you hurt or what you have to destroy to get your way."

One corner of his mouth curled, but it could hardly be called a smile. "It seems as if we are kindred spirits, then."

"No. I *care* about people's feelings. And now I'm going to apologize to Raúl."

"There is no need."

"Of course there is."

"Afraid not, Antonella. You were part of the deal."

"Deal?" She thought her heart would stop as she waited for his answer. How could they make deals that included her? It was impossible. She'd offered herself in marriage, but it had been her choice. Neither of these men owned her, neither could make decisions *for* her.

"Vega Steel will be building in Monterosso. And Monteverde will supply the ore."

"Never," she bit out. It was unthinkable! To sell their ore to Monterosso? So the King could build more tanks and guns in his factories? So the di Savarés could slowly strangle the life from her country? It was the money Monteverde desperately needed, yes, but at what cost?

"You may wish to rethink your position." He sounded mildly friendly, though she knew he was anything but.

Antonella thrust her chin out in answer. "I can't see why we need to."

"One word," he said, his eyes now empty, flat. So cold she hugged herself to ward off a chill. "One very important word: existence."

CHAPTER THREE

"THERE is a storm, Your Highness."

Antonella blinked at the steward as he placed a breakfast tray on a table in her room. She pulled the covers up to her shoulders as she propped herself on an elbow, still groggy after too much worry and too little sleep. "A storm?"

He carefully repositioned the flowers in the small vase on the tray. "Yes, a hurricane. It has swung off track and is coming straight for Canta Paradiso. We are putting to sea very shortly. You may stay aboard if you wish, or you may transfer to the island for a flight out."

"Where is Signor Vega?"

The steward stood at military-like attention. "He was called back to São Paulo on business. He left before daybreak."

Her heart sank. She'd known it was futile, and yet she'd hoped to speak with Raúl once more, hoped to convince him to give Monteverde a chance. Too late now.

No. She would not allow Cristiano di Savaré to defeat her so easily. There was still a very little time left before the loans came due, and she'd spent the night thinking about what Monteverde's next move would be if Raúl would not change his mind. She'd come up with only one solution.

What if Dante went to Montebianco and asked for a loan to get them through this crisis? Their father had nearly started another war when he'd arrested the Crown Princess of that nation, but that was months ago. Would Montebianco help them now? Could she convince her brother to try? She knew he wouldn't want to do it, but it was their last chance.

And if Dante wouldn't approach the King, Antonella would go to Lily and beg her to ask her husband, the Crown Prince, for help. Either way, there was still a chance for them—if she acted quickly.

"Thank you," she said to the steward. "I will go to the airport."

He gave her a formal bow before slipping out of her cabin and closing the door. Antonella bolted from the bed and grabbed her mobile phone. She had to reach Dante. She'd tried last night, but the call wouldn't go through. Perhaps the wind had knocked out a tower.

Or, more likely, something was wrong with Monteverde's communications. They often had trouble with the utility companies as the infrastructure crumbled and there was no money left to repair the aging equipment.

An automated voice informed her that her call could not be completed as dialed and suggested she check the number. She snapped her phone shut and hurried to get dressed. The sooner she was on a plane home, the better.

Antonella emerged onto the top deck of the yacht, in search of someone who could arrange for a launch. She nearly stumbled when she caught sight of the man conversing with the yacht's captain.

Cristiano di Savaré in a tuxedo had been magnificent. But Cristiano in Bermuda shorts, a crisp polo shirt, flip-flops, and Ray-Bans was downright sinful. He looked nothing like a prince and everything like some erotic fantasy of a muscled cabana boy who lived to serve the woman lucky enough to hire him.

He turned at her approach, no doubt because the captain ceased paying attention to him and watched her progress. She could see the captain's eyes moving over her appreciatively, but it was Cristiano's gaze she felt most keenly. Though he wore mirrored sunglasses, she was aware of the burning scrutiny behind them.

She'd dressed in a cotton wrap dress and sported a pair of sandals with a sensible heel. Her hair was pulled into a ponytail, and she'd gone minimal with her make-up. She wasn't trying to attract attention, and yet it never seemed to matter. Attention was what she got.

"You have heard about the storm?" Cristiano said, skipping the preliminaries.

Antonella pushed away a tendril of hair that had escaped her ponytail and blew across her lips. "Yes. When is the launch?" she asked, turning to the captain.

"There is a slight delay," Cristiano said before the captain could reply. "Many in the harbor are requesting transportation."

"I see."

"Have you made flight arrangements yet?"

"No. I had hoped to go straight to the airport and take care of it."

"*Bene.* You may fly with me."

Antonella's pulse beat like the wings of a thousand hummingbirds. The man was unbelievable. "Thank you, but no. I will get a flight when I reach the airport."

Cristiano shoved his shades onto his head. The sunlight had disappeared as clouds rolled into the harbor. His eyes, she realized, weren't blue or gray. They were deep, dark brown.

No, green.

Hazel, that was what it was called. Brown ringed the pupil, but most of the iris was green.

Striking.

How had she missed this at dinner last night? She'd sat across from him, but she'd barely looked directly at him with Raúl sitting beside her. The one time she had, she'd been far more mesmerized by the look on his face than the color of his eyes.

"Antonella," he said sharply.

She jerked. "What?"

"Did you hear me?"

"You were talking about your jet."

"Yes. It's ready, and I have room for you. All commercial flights off the island are booked."

"But you just asked me if I'd made arrangements!"

"I meant last night, before the hurricane changed direction."

She shook her head emphatically. "I'll take my chances at the airport."

Was she crazy? She might despise him, but was it worth putting herself in danger to have the satisfaction of refusing him? Wasn't the most important thing to get back to Monteverde and speak to her brother? If only Dante had been the one to come to Canta Paradiso! He'd have gotten Vega Steel and this would all be moot.

Except he had to stay to hold the country together. And his wife was about to give birth. Antonella had been the only choice, and she'd failed. She wanted to climb back into bed and pull the covers over her head until it all went away.

But she couldn't. Cowardice was not an option.

"Don't be childish," Cristiano snapped.

She forced herself to take a long, slow breath before

speaking. "It's not childish to avoid the company of people you despise."

"No, but it is childish to put yourself in danger because of it."

It was disconcerting to hear her thoughts echoed in his words.

Antonella stared at the mountains rising around the harbor. The airport was on the other side of those mountains. It could take hours to reach at this rate. Dark clouds billowed over the green peaks like a thick blanket unrolling. The wind had already picked up speed in the few hours between the time she'd gone to bed and now.

How she got home didn't matter, so long as she did. "I will fly with you if there is no other option. Though when we reach the airport, I will check to see if I can book a flight first."

"As you wish, *Principessa*."

"But I cannot fly into Monterosso." How would that look? And how would she get home to Monteverde? There were no direct flights, and the border was cut off. A Monteverdian princess could not be ferried across the border by Monterossan soldiers. It was unthinkable.

His expression hardened. "Of course not. We will land in Paris first. You can arrange transport from there."

A dark thought occurred to her. "How do I know you will keep your word? That you won't take me to Monterosso and demand a ransom for my return?"

His voice stroked over her like silk. "If I were to kidnap you, *mia bella*, I could think of far more interesting things to do than demand a ransom."

By the time they were ferried to shore and found a taxi, three hours had passed. Everyone was rushing around the town, trying to batten down the hatches or get off the island. Canta

Paradiso was a private resort island, but there was a town and many residents who lived there full-time. In spite of that, the traffic to the small airport was unbelievable.

Cristiano tucked his cell phone away with a growl. Since the rain had begun, the cell towers had ceased carrying calls for very long. Now, they were dropping altogether. Antonella looked at her signal indicator. No bars.

Cristiano raked a dark-fingered hand through his inky hair. The taxi was small, and his leg lay intimately against hers where they were crowded together in the back seat. At first, she'd tried to move away, but huddling against the door was uncomfortable. She'd struggled for the last hour to pretend that his skin didn't burn into her where they touched.

"Will we make it?" she asked.

He was so close. Close enough that if she simply leaned over a few centimeters, their lips could touch.

And why *would she want to do that?*

"We should. It's just rain thus far. We can still fly out."

"Are you certain?" She watched the rain falling harder outside the steamy window beside him, bit her lip.

His gaze dropped to her mouth. "I am a pilot, *cara*. Rain provides good lift. The wind isn't bad yet, and it also provides lift. There are many hours left before the storm is too dangerous to fly."

"That's good, then."

He leaned back, stretched an arm behind her on the seat. She couldn't escape the contact unless she sat forward. To do so would give him power, so she endured the press of his arm against her shoulders and neck.

The trilling of his phone several minutes later startled her from her reverie. The taxi was warm, and she was so tired that she'd nearly fallen asleep on him. Mortified, she pushed herself as far into her corner of the back seat as she could.

Cristiano answered quickly, before the call dropped again. The swearing that issued from him a few moments later wasn't a good sign.

"What's wrong?" she asked when he finished.

He looked grim. "We're stuck."

"What do you mean, *stuck*?" she asked, trying to tame the note of panic in her voice.

He swore again. "The plane has a hydraulic leak in the brakes. We can't fly without a new cowling, and there isn't one on the island."

Antonella bit back a hysterical laugh. "Is there a chance we can get on a commercial plane?"

"The last flight left twenty minutes ago. There are no more flights in or out today."

"You said it was safe to fly for many hours yet."

"It is. But commercial airlines have different schedules, Antonella. And they've chosen to cancel flights that were coming in later today. Those planes would have been the flights out again."

Antonella stared at him, swallowed the giant lump in her throat. "Now what?"

"We must find a place to stay."

Unbelievable. Could her luck get any worse? "And where do you suggest we look? Do we simply drive up to every hotel on the island and see if they have a vacancy?"

He tapped his phone against his leg. "No, that would take too much time and there are no guarantees. I have another idea."

"And what would that be?"

"I know the man who owns this island. He keeps a villa nearby. We will go there."

She stared at him. "Why didn't you mention this before?"

"I didn't think it would be necessary."

Antonella didn't say anything while he issued instructions to the driver. Maybe she should argue about the practicality of his plan, but what other choice was there? Far better to stay in a private home than be seen together in a hotel. There was always a chance, no matter how remote, that someone from the media would be there and would recognize them. A photo of her with Cristiano di Savaré could do irreparable harm to her country right now.

He put his arm behind her again and she pressed herself farther away from him. He frowned.

"It's no use," he said. "The car is small and there's nowhere to go."

"I realize that, but you don't need to put your arm around me."

"And I thought you liked it when I touched you." His voice contained a hint of sarcasm that irritated her.

"Hardly."

"Then why did you come?"

Antonella blinked. "What choice did I have? You said yourself that all the flights were booked."

"Yes, but to accept help from me of all people…" He tsked.

Antonella saw red. "It wasn't my first choice, no, but I'm not stupid."

His gaze grew sharp, thoughtful. "No, I don't think you are."

"What's that supposed to mean?"

A mocking smile curved his lips. "Whatever you think it means, *Principessa*."

"I think you simply like to irritate me. Why did you offer to help me get off the island if you don't like me so much?"

"I don't have to like you for what I have in mind."

Antonella gasped. "How could you possibly dislike someone and still want to sleep with them?"

The look on his face, something between mildly amused and completely arrogant, sent heat flooding into her cheeks. Had she mistaken his meaning?

"There is a fine line between hate and passion, Antonella," he replied. "One sometimes makes the other more rich."

"That's horrible." She'd always thought, assuming she weren't obligated to marry a man of her father's choosing, she would have to like the man she slept with for the first time. She'd never expected to have that choice, however. Now that it seemed she might, she was more than a little appalled at her physical reaction to Cristiano.

He quirked an eyebrow. "Really? You would expect me to believe a woman of your experience has liked every man she's ever bedded?"

Her jaw clenched. She should have realized where this conversation would go. "I prefer not to discuss this with you."

"Why not? Ashamed?"

"Of course not!"

"So how many has it been, Antonella? How many men have you lured to your bed?" He looked haughty, cruel. It made her furious.

"Lured? *Lured*? You make me sound like I'm running a stall at the market! *Come get your peaches, come get your plums—hurry before they're all gone.*"

His expression seemed in danger of crumpling for a split second. She thought he might laugh, but he turned and looked out the window at the rain, ignoring her. He also didn't move his arm. Fury cycled through her in waves until she decided *the hell with it* and flopped back on the seat, wedging him over where he took too much of her space.

What a hypocrite!

His body was hard, solid, and hot. Antonella folded her arms over her chest and leaned her head back—on his arm since he hadn't moved it. He infuriated her with his accusations. He knew nothing about her, and yet he smugly thought he knew everything.

Arrogant man!

He took up all the air in the taxi. She wanted to roll down the window and stick her head out, but it was raining too hard. She was just so tired. So damn tired. As her temper deflated, her eyes drifted closed in spite of the effort she made to keep them open.

Cristiano's scent wrapped around her senses. He smelled like rain and spice, and a pang of sadness pierced her. Why? It took her a moment to realize that it reminded her of something out of her childhood. Was it when her mother had fixed spiced tea for her when she was sick?

Yes, that was it. Spice equaled comfort back then. She could picture her mother as if it were yesterday—her sad, beautiful mother who'd died far earlier than she should have. Was that when her father had grown violent?

She couldn't remember. She'd always tried to block those memories. Like the time he'd squeezed the life from Dante's gerbil because Dante had forgotten to feed it. Her brother, who'd been ten at the time—far older than her impressionable five years—had taken the incident stoically.

Antonella had cried and cried. It was the first time she'd ever experienced such cruelty. She'd never forgotten it, used to burst into tears at the oddest times when the memory crashed in on her. Even years later.

Her face was suddenly cool, and she realized it was the air against her wet cheeks.

No, not now. Please, not now.

She opened her eyes, blinked against the blur. Then she swiped her hands over her cheeks, trying to stop the flow before Cristiano noticed and mocked her. She hadn't cried over that memory in so long she couldn't even remember the last time.

"Crying won't work," Cristiano said coldly—but his voice sounded oddly thick.

Antonella turned away from him. She didn't want him to be here, didn't want him to become a part of her struggle to be a normal person. It wasn't his business! Nothing in her life was his business. "I'm just tired. Leave me alone."

Would she never be free of this? Would episodes from her past always move her to tears when she least expected it? She felt weak, helpless—and angry. Sometimes, in these moments, she thought she could kill her father if he were in front of her and at her mercy.

And she hated that feeling most of all. The tears came faster now, turned into gulping sobs. She couldn't stop the memories, couldn't stop the guilt. She should have done something, should have—

Cristiano swore, then wrapped his arms around her and pulled her against him.

"No, let me go," she begged, trying to rip his hands away from her body. "Let me *go*."

But he didn't. He turned her toward him, cupped the back of her head and pressed her to his chest. She bucked against him, trying to get away, but he was too strong. Eventually, her shoulders slumped.

And once she gave up, his grip softened, his hand rubbing rhythmically up and down her neck while he spoke to her softly. She strained to hear the words over the roar of the rain and wind outside, over her own crying, and realized it was a song.

A song.

Shock was the least of what she felt at that moment. It was such an oddly tender gesture, and from the last person in the world she would have expected it. It was as if he understood somehow.

Her fisted hands curled into his shirt, held tight as she worked hard to stop the tears. She had every reason to hate him, but in that moment he was her ally. He held her for what seemed like hours. It was the closest she'd felt to anyone in a very long time.

CHAPTER FOUR

THE taxi took them to the villa located on a remote beach. By the time they reached the house, Antonella's tears had dried and she'd pushed away from Cristiano again. Fresh embarrassment buffeted her in waves. How could she have lost control like that? And with him, of all people? His shirt was wrinkled where she'd crumpled it in her fist, and a hint of mascara smudged the white fabric, but Cristiano said nothing.

Madonna mia. If the owner took them in, she was locking herself in a bedroom and not coming out again until the storm was over. The less time she spent in Cristiano's company, the better.

Antonella waited in the car while Cristiano went to the door and checked to see if the island tycoon was home. He wasn't, and yet a few minutes later Cristiano had managed to somehow get a call through to the man in New York.

"The staff is on holiday," he said when he returned to the taxi, "but we are welcome to stay until the storm has passed. There is a caretaker in the cottage we drove by. He will let us in."

"Wouldn't we be better off in town?" Despite her earlier relief at not going to a hotel, she suddenly preferred it to being alone with this man for the foreseeable future. She felt too exposed, too raw. She couldn't keep up the barrier of strength she needed simply to be in his company. It was like living on a battlefield.

Cristiano seemed oblivious to her torment. "If others were turned away at the airport, then the hotels could be full."

Antonella reached for her phone, hoping she had a signal. "We can call and check." At least in a hotel, there'd be other people. And maybe even rooms on different floors. She wouldn't have to see him at all. When the airport reopened, she could be on a flight out without ever talking to him again.

He frowned. "We have a safe place to stay, *cara*. And our driver would probably like to return to his home before the worst hits, yes? There is not a lot of time left for error."

A sinking feeling settled over her like a veil. She hadn't thought of that. The driver glanced at her in the rear-view mirror, his eyes darting away a second later. He was young, perhaps had a wife and small children waiting in a tidy house somewhere. And he'd driven her and Cristiano through the rain-swept streets for two hours now.

"Of course," Antonella said. As much as she wanted to get away from Cristiano, she couldn't endanger anyone to do so. They may be alone here, but she didn't need to spend more than a few moments in his company. It would be fine.

Fifteen minutes later, they'd located the caretaker, gotten a key, and let themselves into the house. The place was big, but not as sprawling and opulent as one would expect. It was furnished island-style, with low sea-grass couches, bamboo floors, simple woven rugs, and bright tropical prints interspersed with monochromatic tones. Antonella walked through to the huge kitchen at the back of the house and gazed out at the landscape. A wall of French windows overlooked a patio and pool that gave way to a long stretch of manicured lawn. The lawn sloped down to a retaining wall several hundred meters away. Below that was an extensive swath of white beach. The sky was pale with rain, and palm trees lashed over double in the wind. The ocean that had been turquoise and lapis only yesterday was now grey and roiling. White caps foamed across the surface.

She stood very still, watching and listening. Slowly, it occurred to her that the muted roar echoing through the house came from the wind cleaving around the structure. The power of it was staggering, and nothing like she'd ever experienced before.

"I put us in the master bedroom."

Antonella bit back a scream of surprise and spun to face Cristiano. She hadn't heard him approach. He looked like a beach bum standing in the shadowy entry to the kitchen. A gorgeous beach bum.

He disconcerted her. Too much.

"*Us*? Are you hard of hearing? I said last night I'm not sleeping with you."

He came into the room like a cat—silent, muscles bunching and flowing with oiled grace. She realized he was wet when the meager light hit him. He stripped off the polo shirt in a smooth motion, wiped it across his face, and then dropped it on the marble-topped island that ran the length of the room.

Antonella's breath caught. She had to force her lungs to work as she blanked her expression. Every inch of him was corded with muscle, as if he were a day laborer instead of a prince. Broad shoulders and defined pecs tapered to a narrow waist and lean hips. His skin was tanned, and yet it grew lighter the lower her eyes went. A dark arrow of hair slipped beneath the loose waistband of his shorts, and she found herself wanting to follow it down, see the rest of him.

Antonella snapped her gaze to his face. He smirked as if he knew exactly what she'd been thinking.

"You know you want to."

Antonella blinked. "Want to what?"

The smirk turned into a grin. "Sleep with me. In the master bedroom."

Oh, dear God—

She shook her head, heat suffusing her face. "No, I don't and I won't. I'm taking one of the other bedrooms—there *are* other bedrooms, yes?"

Cristiano shuffled past her, gazed out the window. She refused to focus on his naked back, the taut muscles of his buttocks beneath the damp material of his shorts—

"There are," he said, turning to face her again. "But I just checked the generator and the fuel is nearly spent. Someone forgot to fill it, or it's been drained recently. If we lose power, there'll be no light."

"Surely there are candles. Have you looked?"

"Not yet, but yes, there must be. And yet we need to preserve those as well. Not to mention there are trees outside the front of the home. The other bedrooms are up there. If a tree fell onto the house, then what? I prefer not to have to dig you out, assuming you survived."

Antonella shuddered, but whether it was over the picture of a tree crushing her or being forced to share a room with this man, she didn't know.

"One of us can stay in the living area. There are couches, the floor—"

"And should we lose power, or should something happen to this house, we would be separated. It is best to stay together, Antonella."

She folded her arms. "How can you possibly know that? We don't have hurricanes or cyclones—or whatever you call them—where we come from."

"Every Monterossan prince since the beginning of time has

served in the army, *Principessa*." His eyes grew hard, bleak. She swallowed. "I assure you I have endured things you cannot imagine. Trust me when I say I know of what I speak."

She did believe him, and yet she was still unnerved by the prospect of spending so much time confined with him. "Very convenient, Cristiano. I am forced to share a room with you, it would seem."

"What is your alternative?"

"I don't suppose I have one, do I?"

"Not if you care to survive."

He spoke so casually it chilled her. Antonella went to the window, touched her fingers to the pane of glass as the water chased down it outside. "How much worse will the storm get?"

He came and stood beside her. She glanced up at his profile as he stared out at the churning sea, his expression troubled. Tried resolutely not to look down at all that naked skin.

"I wish I knew. It will worsen as it spins toward land. Possibly a category four when it comes ashore." His head tilted back as he looked up at the sky. "The wind will reach one hundred and thirty-five knots, perhaps."

"I don't know what that means."

He turned to face her. She kept her gaze straight ahead, though she could see him quite well in her peripheral vision. He was too close, too big. His bare skin gleamed in the pale light, and drops of water fell from his head onto his chest, trickled down, down….

"In excess of two hundred kilometers an hour."

Antonella's stomach dropped. She turned without thinking, took an instinctive step backward to put distance between them. "W-what could happen to us? Are we safe here?"

He perused her body in a leisurely way before answering, as if he knew she was as disconcerted by his nakedness as she was by the storm. "The trees could be a problem, and we will probably lose power. Beyond that, I do not know."

"What about the sea?"

"The drop to the ocean is steep, so a storm surge is not likely."

Antonella hurried to the center island and opened the handbag she'd set there. Her cell phone had no signal. She dropped it into her purse again. "Do you have a signal?"

He sauntered toward her, pulled his phone from his shorts. "No."

Antonella leaned against the counter for support and closed her eyes. "I should have kept trying to call Dante. He will worry."

"Perhaps he will simply think you are too occupied with your lover to inform him of your movements."

She stiffened. "I call my brother every day."

Why did she feel the need to justify herself?

"Do you? How extraordinary."

"You don't speak with your family daily?"

His laugh was unexpected. Disbelieving. "No. I am thirty-one, *cara*. My father doesn't expect a regular report."

"Dante doesn't expect a report either. But we are close, and much has happened recently—" She broke off, unwilling to continue. No one knew what she and Dante had suffered over the years at the hands of their father.

No one would, because neither of them was talking about it. Perhaps Dante had shared his story with his wife, but Antonella did not know and would not ask.

"It is good you are close," Cristiano said after a moment. "Very good."

She wasn't certain how he meant that, but a shiver crept along her nerve endings. He turned and started rummaging through drawers. The rattle of silverware grated on her after a few moments and she knew she had to do something or go insane.

"What can I do?" She could've started searching for candles, but it was best if they didn't duplicate effort. Since he seemed to know what to expect from the storm, she would bow to his experience.

If only he'd put on a shirt! Perhaps she could think then. Perhaps this shivery, achy feeling would go away. She'd seen bare-chested men before, but that had usually been poolside. Cristiano, naked to the waist, in a kitchen—

She closed her eyes. When she opened them again, he was looking at her.

"I need you to fill all the sinks and bath tubs with water," he said after a few moments of silence in which she was utterly convinced he knew the effect he was having and did his utmost to draw it out.

She blinked. "Why?"

"Because if we lose power, we lose water."

It made sense, but she'd have never thought of it until too late.

He continued, "Next, see if you can find any flashlights, batteries, candles and matches. If you run across a radio, get that too. Take everything to the master bedroom and leave it. I'll search in here for a few things, and then I'm going outside to close the shutters. If you could get some towels and leave them on the kitchen island, I'll use this entrance."

She bit her lip as she studied him. He was all business now, and nothing like she'd expected. Dante was the most practical person she knew, and yet this man made him look like a cosseted child in comparison. At the moment, he was more like a military commando than an heir to a throne.

"Do you really think it could get that bad?"

His expression was grave. "Anything is possible, *Principessa*. It's best to be prepared."

* * *

Cristiano was soaked. He'd spent twenty minutes in the pouring rain, closing the shutters and hooking them. The caretaker should have done the job when the storm had first been reported to have swung off track, but the man seemed to do little besides sit in his house and watch television.

Cristiano took no satisfaction in knowing it was unlikely the man was watching anything now. The rain was coming down so hard that the satellite signal had gone out a while ago. He knew because he'd turned on the flat-panel television in the bedroom before he'd gone outside. Now, he stood in the kitchen and stripped out of his shorts. Antonella was nowhere to be seen, but at least she'd brought the towels.

A vision of her face, her eyes red and swollen, came to him. He resolutely shoved it away.

He could *not* feel sorry for her.

She was a Monteverdian *and* a Romanelli. And he had a job to do. A promise to keep.

He'd sworn on Julianne's memory that he would put an end to this war if it were the last thing he did. His people needed peace. Too long they'd lived in the shadow of this conflict.

He owed it to them. To her. He should have been there. If he had, he could have stopped her from dying. Could have kept her out of that convoy. He mourned the loss of all who'd died, but he didn't feel responsible for them the way he did for his wife.

Dio, he should have never married her.

He grabbed a towel, scrubbed it over his body. He tried to picture Julianne, to remember the exact curve of her smile, but his mind insisted on seeing another face.

Antonella's.

He couldn't deny that he wanted her. He knew she was a thoughtless, manipulative *puttana*, yet he couldn't seem to overrule the urges of his body. He *should* be able to do so, but he couldn't.

She got to him on more than a physical level. When she'd cried earlier, he'd felt as if someone had stabbed a serrated knife into him and twisted it. He'd held her close and sung the same song his mother sang when he'd been small and unwilling to go to sleep.

Why?

Because something about Antonella defied explanation. She was shrewd and tough, manipulative—and yet there was pain, the kind of pain that only came with depth of experience. He knew because he'd felt that kind of pain too. He recognized something of himself within her.

And he didn't like it one bit. To feel any sympathy at all for her, any kinship, was a betrayal of his dead wife's memory. Not because she was a woman—he'd had plenty of lovers over the past few years—but because she was a Monteverdian.

Cristiano tossed the soaked towel aside and prepared to grab a fresh one to wrap around his waist when a squeak from the entry hall drew his attention. Antonella stood there, her dark hair pulled away from her face, her jaw hanging loose as she stared at him. His body started to react to her perusal.

He didn't care. Let her see the effect she had on him. Surely she was accustomed to it. Hell, she probably expected it.

Maybe, just maybe, if he got this physical attraction for her out of the way, he could think again. Could push her to agree to his plan and get on with the business of taking over her country.

A second later, she pivoted on her heel and disappeared in a rush. She seemed flustered—and yet it was an act. Had to be. She *wanted* him to feel pity for her, to feel protective. She'd already succeeded once today.

He cinched the towel low over his hips. He'd been insane to consider, even for a moment, that this sultry princess— the woman who'd been draped over Raúl Vega last night— was anything other than what overwhelming evidence indicated she was.

She did *not* defy explanation. She was a beautiful woman who enjoyed her pleasures. Aside from her two royal engagements, she'd been linked with one fashion designer, a German count, three Formula One drivers, and an aging Italian billionaire among others. Raúl Vega was only her latest conquest.

Cristiano had spent a lot of money and effort to confirm the rumors of Monteverde's financial crisis. His father believed that if they waited, Monteverde would fall like a domino into their hands.

But Cristiano was taking no chances; he would allow no eleventh hour rescues. Now that he'd dried up the last source of possible investment, what remained of his plan was simple enough: his money for Antonella's cooperation in gaining the mineral rights to Monteverde's ore deposits. With the ore under Monterossan control, he could enforce peace in the region.

It was their last bankable resource. If he controlled it, he controlled them.

Yet he knew his plan wasn't as straightforward as he'd first thought. She was shrewder than he'd imagined, for one thing. Antonella would never allow herself to be bought so cheaply. No, what she would expect was the crown of Monterosso.

And he would offer it to her on a platter if necessary.

But he would never deliver it. To go through with a marriage, to her of all people, was out of the question. She would be humiliated, perhaps, but it wouldn't last. She'd already survived two royal breakups. A third wouldn't shatter her.

He glanced up at the roof as a gust of wind howled along

the structure. He'd expected trouble, but not this kind. While the storm had worked to his advantage in isolating Antonella, it was bad for every other reason known to man.

Cristiano pulled open a drawer and found a roll of utility tape. The patio doors were the only ones with no exterior shutters. The addition was new, and though there was an overhang, he didn't trust that would be enough to protect the glass. Once he finished taping the windows in long spokes across the glass—if they shattered, at least the tape would help prevent shards from going everywhere—he padded toward the bedroom to face his adversary.

Antonella sat in a chair in one corner, flipping through a magazine. She did not look up as he entered. "Is it any worse?" she asked.

Cristiano unzipped his bag and pulled out some dry clothes. "Not yet, but I think it soon will be. Did you find a radio?"

"Yes, but no extra batteries."

They would have to be careful listening to updates once the power failed. "There isn't much food in the house. Crackers, sausage, a jar of olives, aerosol cheese—"

"What's aerosol cheese?"

She'd looked up, her brows drawing together. A moment later, she seemed to realize what she'd done. Her eyes darted to the towel cinched low on his hips, back up again. When her tongue swept over her lower lip, Cristiano thought his body would turn to stone. As it was, the towel was about to reveal her effect on him.

Dio santo.

He clamped down on his will, forced his body to behave. "It is an American product," he said matter-of-factly. He made a motion with his hand. "You spray it on the crackers."

"Spray?" She looked horrified.

"*Si.*"

A shudder passed over her. "That sounds perfectly vile."

"Depends on how hungry you are and how long until your next meal." Though he'd been born into privilege, he'd done his time with the Monterossan Special Forces. He understood deprivation and hunger quite well. While she flitted around her family palazzo, beautiful and elegant, her countrymen—and women—huddled in bunkers on the border, surrounded by artillery and razor wire, and ate meals out of a package. Just like he and the soldiers he'd served with had done.

"We should have returned to town," she said, pushing up out of the chair and pacing toward the shuttered windows. She spun around again before she reached them. "Then we wouldn't be isolated out here with *spray cheese* and no communications with the outside world."

"Be thankful we are in a safe place, *Principessa*. There are those in the world who are not."

If she noticed the steel in his voice, she didn't show it. She seemed oblivious, on edge. Did the storm frighten her that much?

Her gaze raked over him, almost wild-eyed, then skittered away again. Once more, she spun toward the windows, following the track she'd paced before.

Cristiano recognized someone on the edge of control when he saw it. But what was causing her to feel so skittish? Did she have a thing about closed in spaces? Not that the room was small, but with the shutters closed and only a lamp for light, it felt rather cave-like.

Or was it the fact he was nearly naked? An interesting thought, to be sure.

"It wouldn't have mattered where we were. Phone calls can fix nothing right now. And there was no time to make the trek back to town. This is the best we could do."

She stopped and put her head in her hands. "I cannot believe I am stuck here with you for the foreseeable future. This is a nightmare."

"I can think of a few ways to make the time pass." He said it primarily because he knew it would irritate her.

Her head snapped up again. *Score.* "This isn't something to make jokes about."

"What makes you think I'm joking?"

She turned away from him with something that sounded like a growl. She made the circuit to the window again, stopped. Spun around, hands on hips, breasts thrust out enticingly. "Get this in your head, Cristiano—I am *not* sleeping with you. And I'd appreciate it very much if you'd put something *on*."

Her voice rose at the end. Cristiano absently rubbed a hand over his chest, enjoying himself tremendously. So she *was* rattled by his semi-nakedness. Because she wanted him, no doubt. And because she felt guilty for doing so.

He certainly understood the feeling. "Do I disturb you, *mia bella*?"

She stood so stiffly, like a nun who'd blundered into a strip club. Now, why was that a turn-on? She wasn't a virgin, wasn't naïve, and yet she carried off the act so well. The contrast with her sensual body intrigued him. Made him hard. She couldn't help but know it, clad as he was in a towel.

Her throat moved. "Don't be ridiculous," she rasped. A moment later, she waved a hand airily as she seemed to gather her equilibrium. "You don't affect me one way or the other. So you might as well put on some clothes."

The corners of his mouth curled in a smile that was both evil and triumphant. "I think you are right."

And then he dropped the towel.

CHAPTER FIVE

ANTONELLA fought hard not to shriek and spin away like a frightened virgin. No, she had to play this cool. Collected. He thought she was experienced—so experienced she must act.

But Cristiano di Savaré was the first man she'd ever seen naked in the flesh, and the sight affected her quite oddly. She felt dizzy for one thing. Like she needed to sit before her knees buckled.

And she felt hot. Prickles of heat skittered along her skin like tiny flames, scorching everything in their path. Her mouth dropped, snapped shut again.

He was…was…*big*…all over. And completely unabashed.

The towel lay heaped at his feet, forgotten. His eyes glittered, daring her to react.

Every line of him was beautiful. His skin was smooth and golden, yet lighter from a point above his groin to the tops of his thighs. Inanely, she thought he must spend a lot of time outside without a shirt.

Her eyes skimmed downward, hardly believing what she was seeing and yet unable to look away at the same time. His penis thrust out from his body proudly. She understood enough about male anatomy to know what an erect penis meant. But why? That part she didn't understand. How could he be aroused? They'd been arguing, for pity's sake!

Another, more frightening thought occurred to her: should she be scared of him? They were alone here, just the two of them and a storm outside.

He was bigger than she was, stronger. It was in his blood to hate her, just as it was in hers to hate him. Would he use his size and strength against her, take what he wanted by force? No one would come to her rescue if she screamed.

Her mind cast about frantically for solutions, ways in which she could fight him off if he attacked her.

"Want to help?" he said, his voice a sensual purr as he slowly reached for the clothing he'd tossed onto the bed.

Antonella drew in a shaky breath. No, she did not think he would force himself on her. He'd soothed her in the taxi when he could have ignored her. She kept telling herself that for comfort as she turned away very deliberately, very carefully. She couldn't let him know she was flustered—or frightened. She couldn't give him that kind of power.

Somehow she made her legs work. She returned to the slipper chair, sank down on it and picked up the magazine she'd been thumbing through. Thought better of flipping pages when she realized her hands were shaking. She laid the magazine on her lap and opened it to a random page, pretended to study what was there.

Cristiano hadn't moved to follow her, yet he was still naked. Still aroused. Fear seeped away, replaced by heat and the pain of her own desire. Odd. She'd never realized sexual arousal could hurt.

Her heartbeat pounded in her chest, her neck, her wrists. She wanted to go into the bathroom and sink down into the cold water she'd filled the tub with. Perhaps then the heat would go away.

"I take it that's a no," Cristiano said.

Her cheeks were already on fire, but that didn't stop the heat of a fresh blush. She'd forgotten he'd spoken to her, had asked her a question. She'd been so flustered by his body, by her own thoughts, that she'd blanked.

Did he know? Should she answer him now, or play it cool?

She saw movement in her periphery, but refused to look up. A flash of something pale. Clothing, she hoped. Please God, let him cover that body up before she made a bigger fool of herself. Before he realized she was a stammering virgin seeing her first naked man. Somehow, she knew that would diminish her in his eyes. He would pity her then. She couldn't take his pity again today. Didn't want it.

"Too bad, Antonella," he said. The sound of a zipper going up nearly made her breathe a very audible sigh of relief. "The time would pass so pleasantly. Before you know it, we'd be leaving again."

"Oh yes," she forced out. Without looking up, of course. "We'd be leaving. And you'd waste no time informing everyone you could think of that you'd bedded me."

"I never kiss and tell, *Principessa*."

"Of course not," she said, letting him know with her tone that she didn't believe a word of it.

"But if I want to claim we've been lovers, what's to stop me?"

Her head snapped back as her eyes met his. He was wearing another pair of khaki shorts and a navy T-shirt that molded the shape of his chest and abdomen. He was clothed, and yet her pulse still zipped along like an express train.

"You wouldn't. Besides, I would deny it."

Cristiano laughed. "Who would believe you, *bellissima*? You have a reputation, shall we say?"

Antonella's cheeks burned. Oh, yes, she had a reputation—

gained when men had *lied* about her, as this one threatened
to do. It made her angry. She flipped a page in the magazine,
ripping the paper as she did so. *Damn him.*

But maybe she could fight back. She arched an eyebrow,
affected as chilly a look as she could manage. "Perhaps they
would believe it when I claimed you were not so good as *your*
reputation? I could say you were a selfish and *hasty*—" she
emphasized the word "—lover."

Cristiano's laugh was louder this time. Then he swept her
with hot eyes. "You are welcome to try."

Antonella slapped the magazine closed irritably. "This is
ridiculous, Cristiano. We could be in very real danger, and yet
you keep insulting me and making jokes."

His expression grew serious. "Do you know what I think?"

"No, but I know you will tell me."

He came over to where she sat, towered above her until he
dropped to one knee and reached for her. Her heart stopped,
simply stopped, as she tried to imagine what he was about to
do. He picked up the magazine, turned it and set it back down.

"I think you want me very much, Antonella."

She forced herself to speak past the giant lump in her
throat. "You are deluded," she managed.

"Am I?" He stood and moved away without waiting for a
reply.

Antonella watched numbly as he disappeared through the
door that connected the bedroom with the rest of the house.
Then she looked down. And realized that he'd turned the
magazine the correct way.

She'd been staring at it upside down the entire time.

By the time Cristiano returned a short while later, she'd
managed to calm her racing heart and jangled nerves. She'd
tried reading a book, but the power had blinked a few times

and then snapped out, leaving her in the dark. She'd fumbled for the candle she'd placed on the table nearby, cursing softly when it rolled away and fell.

Before she could get down on her hands and knees to find it, Cristiano was there, shining a flashlight into the darkness. He retrieved one of the candles from the stash at the foot of the bed and lit it, then switched off the light. A second later, he was stretched out on the bed, leaning against the headboard with his hands behind his head. The pose molded the shirt to his chest, bulged the muscles in his arms. Made him seem so delicious and sexy.

Antonella crossed her arms over her body protectively and concentrated on the flickering candle where he'd set it on the bedside table. Anything except look at him.

"It will be a very long night if we ignore each other," Cristiano finally said.

She forced herself to gaze at him evenly. "It's already been a long day. Interminable."

"Yes."

Her pride pricked at the idea that he found her company tiresome. Why? Wasn't that what she'd just intimated about him?

"Tell me about Monteverde," he said, and her jaw threatened to fall to the floor.

"Why?" she asked a moment later, suspicion curling around the edges of her awareness.

"Because we are alone, the night is long, and it's a good topic."

"Why not tell me about Monterosso?"

He shrugged. "If you wish."

For the next twenty minutes, he told her about his country—about the green mountains, the black cliffs, and the azure ocean. She found herself listening intently, nodding from time to time as she realized how much Monterosso sounded like Monterverde. When he talked of cool forests and bubbling mountain streams, she could picture them perfectly. When he spoke of the dryness along the coast, the cacti and aloe plants, she felt as if she'd stood beside him and looked upon the same things.

"It's amazing," she said when he finished.

"I think so, yes."

Antonella shook her head. "No, I mean it sounds exactly like Monteverde."

He arched an eyebrow. "You are surprised? We were a single country once."

"And you would wish it so again," she said, inflecting her words with steel.

"Have I said that?"

"You didn't have to. It's what your people have wanted for years."

"Is this your opinion, or what you've been told by your father and brother?" His voice was diamond-edged.

"If it's not what Monterosso wants, why must we defend our border? Why are your tanks and guns there? Your soldiers?"

"Because yours are."

My God, men were insane. Was this the sort of circular logic that had caused so many lives to be lost over the years? While the solution seemed obvious, she knew it wasn't. "Then why don't we both turn around and go home?"

"Because we don't trust each other, Antonella."

She sat up straighter in her chair. "But we could sign treaties, pledge to cooperate—"

His laughter startled her. "Do you not think this has been tried?"

"It hasn't been tried since Dante became King. We have only the ceasefire—"

"How would this change anything? He is a Romanelli."

"What is that supposed to mean? That he is untrustworthy? That *we* are not as good as the di Savarés?"

"It means that your word and your treaties have not been enough thus far. Why should we believe your brother any different from your father?"

She ached to tell him. And yet she couldn't. Because it was unexplainable. And private. No, what she and Dante had endured wouldn't convince this man. And there was every danger it would only reinforce his beliefs. Abuse often turned out abusers. For all Cristiano knew, Dante could be just like his predecessor.

"He simply is," she said firmly.

"Yes," Cristiano sneered, "this is quite enough to convince me of Monteverdian sincerity."

"You have yet to prove you are any better. If you would turn your tanks around, pull back your soldiers—"

"And let you bomb innocent civilians?" Rage suddenly seemed to roll from him in a giant wave. It was so palpable she thought it would crush her. His expression was dark, hard.

Intimidating.

Her voice came out in a whisper in spite of her best effort to make it otherwise. "We don't use bombs against civilians. We only defend ourselves against Monterossan hostility—"

His laughter was so sharp and bitter it sliced her off in midsentence. She stared at him, at his jaw that had turned to granite. At the bleakness he failed to hide.

A moment later, he shoved both hands through his hair, blew out a hard breath. "You are quite wrong about that," he said, his voice so utterly controlled it chilled her. He'd gone from hot rage to cold hatred in the space of a breath.

"I-I don't believe you." But her heart pounded in her throat.

Could it be true? Her father had been capable of ordering such cruelty. More than capable. She thought of Dante's pet gerbil, swallowed. *No, don't let me cry again. Not now.*

"It is quite true, I assure you," he said, his demeanor smooth. She had the impression he'd just fought a battle with himself and won. A dark, cold battle that she didn't understand.

"How do you know this? How can you prove it?"

"I don't have to prove it. I carry the results in my heart every day of my life."

"You were…hurt?" She couldn't imagine it. His body, as much as she'd seen of it, was perfect. If he'd been hurt, surely there would be signs of it. Or had he lost someone?

"My wife, *Principessa*. She was killed on an aid mission to the border. A roadside bomb blew up under the truck she was riding in."

Her chest squeezed tight as her lungs refused to work properly. "I'm sorry," she managed. She'd known his wife died shortly after their marriage, but she'd never known how it happened. She'd only had true freedom of information for a few months now. Before that, her father had tightly controlled the news she'd been exposed to.

A bomb. My God, how horrible. The poor woman.

Poor Cristiano.

Could her father have supported such a thing? Known about it? *Ordered* it? The thought made her shiver.

"Of course you are." The words were perfunctory, yet each felt like a physical blow.

"I *am* sorry, Cristiano," she insisted. "I've lost loved ones too."

Her mother, her aunt Maria. Leni, her first dog.

"Have you?" His voice was still so cold. "Yet you always manage to find someone new to replace the old."

Her heart hurt. It simply hurt. He believed her the worst kind of monster. The kind of woman who cared for no one but herself, who was unaffected by the pain of others. Why that bothered her, she wasn't certain. But it did.

The tears she'd been holding back threatened to consume her. *No, she would not cry. She would not give him the satisfaction. His opinion meant nothing.*

She got to her feet, her arms wrapped around her body to ward off the ice that hung in the air despite the tropical heat. He wanted to lash out—she understood that. Understood the need to hurt someone when you were hurting.

Yet how did that make him any different from other men she had known? From her father?

It didn't. Cristiano hit with words instead of fists. And the pain was worse in some ways. Psychological pain had repercussions beyond the physical that stayed with you forever. She'd learned that lesson long ago. Hell, she was still learning it. Dante's gerbil was a prime example.

And she was far too tired of it to suffer a moment's more abuse at his, or anyone's, hands.

"Where are you going?" he demanded as she crossed to the bedroom door.

She turned, her head held high, tears in check for the moment. "It doesn't seem to matter where I stay, does it, Cristiano? There is danger for me in every room of this house. So I think I will take my chances in another room for a while."

Cristiano bowed his head and concentrated on breathing evenly. He should not have spoken of Julianne's death to her. But he'd felt the darkness settling over him when she'd accused Monterosso of prolonging the hostilities, and he'd been unable to keep it at bay. He'd wanted to wound, just like he'd been wounded by the guilt of causing an innocent woman to die. A woman whose only crime had been to marry him.

He had to go after Antonella. He couldn't let her wander through the house with the storm intensifying. A tree could crash down on them. Windows could shatter. He could be wrong about the depth of the ocean and a storm surge could sweep into the house and drag her away.

Death lay over the structure like a coiled serpent, simply waiting for an opportunity to strike.

And he couldn't let that happen. He needed her if he wanted to put an end to the violence.

No.

He tilted his head back on the headboard and sighed. It was more than that. She was a person, and though he might not trust her or like her very much, she didn't deserve anything less than his best care for her safety while they endured this storm.

It had gotten out of control so fast.

He'd only meant to find out a bit more about her, but he should have known the conversation would head down a road he did not want to go. Could a Monteverdian and a Monterossan truly spend time together and not fight about the problems between their countries? If it were possible, perhaps there would be peace already.

Still, he was here to make sure it happened. He had to control his emotions and he had to deal with Antonella like a rational man, not a wounded lion.

He pushed away from the bed, grabbing the flashlight, and headed through the door. Outside, the wind howled and moaned. Tree branches scraped across the terracotta roof with an eerie sound like fingernails against a chalkboard. The walls groaned and creaked.

"Antonella!"

She didn't answer, so he passed through the hall and into the living room. She wasn't there. Next, he went into the kitchen. The temperature in the house was starting to climb now that the power had gone out. He would have to open a window soon, though he did not want to for fear of the wind being so strong. But they would need fresh air. Sweat beaded on his skin as he moved through the structure.

"Antonella!" She couldn't have gone far, but she probably couldn't hear him over the wind. He went into the first bedroom, shone the light. Nothing. The second also yielded nothing.

The third time, as the beam swept across the room, he hit the jackpot. She lay on the bed, curled into a ball, a pillow hugged tight to her body. The sight shafted an arrow of regret straight through his chest.

She looked like a child, vulnerable and helpless, and his protective instincts were kicking into gear. *Dio*, he had to remember who she was. What she was. They'd been here a handful of hours and he was already going soft.

"Antonella," he said over the wind and rain pelting the roof.

"Go away."

"It's not safe in here. We have to return to the master bedroom."

She bolted into an upright position, her hair wild as she shoved it out of her face. Her eyes were red-rimmed. "It's not safe in there either," she shot back. "I'll take my chances here."

"Don't be stupid. We're going back."

He started forward and she scrambled against the headboard, folding her knees against her body as if to ward him off.

"It won't work, *Principessa*," he said, exasperation and

fury surging through him in twin waves. His instincts were sounding an alarm inside his head, telling him to get her and get out, no matter how hard she fought. The skin at the back of his neck prickled as the wind surged against the house, banging the shutters. He'd closed them, but they were old and somewhat loose in places. "I'm bigger and stronger; I *will* win."

Her eyes widened as he reached for her. She looked a little scared at his intensity, but he had no time to play nice. He had to get them back to safety. As if to punctuate the point, there was a loud snap outside. The wind howled even louder.

He grabbed her foot and yanked her toward him. She screamed.

But he ignored her feminine hysterics and dragged her up into his grasp. She twisted like a cat. "No!"

Cristiano gripped her shoulders hard and shook her. "Stop fighting me," he ordered. "We have to go."

But she didn't seem to be listening. She twisted again, fell to the bed as he lost his hold on her. He lunged for her, furious—and more than a little concerned at the crackling sound coming from above their heads.

"We have to go," he repeated. "Now."

Instead of cooperating, she flinched and covered her head as if he were about to strike her. The sight gave him pause. He'd never hit a woman in his life. Never had a woman cower from him as if he were about to do so. Did she really think…?

Why?

Why?

Another sharp crack outside dragged his attention up. A moment later, the roof split open. Terracotta and splintered wood crumbled through the opening, showering down around them.

No time left.

Acting on a surge of adrenaline and pure instinct, Cristiano grabbed Antonella and hauled her from the bed. There was just enough time to roll her beneath him before the wall opened under the weight of the tree like a zipper dragging downward.

CHAPTER SIX

WHEN Antonella came to, the first thing she noticed was the heavy weight pressing down on her. She could barely breathe. The second was the sharp smell of rain and the dark odor of wet wood. Wind whipped in gusts against her body, chilling where her dress was soaked through. She tried to push the weight off, but it shifted. Suddenly, she was looking up into Cristiano's dark face.

Her heart turned over at the sight of blood trickling down his cheek.

"You are not hurt?" he said before she could manage to speak.

"I-I don't think so. But I can't breathe," she rasped.

He shifted to the side and Antonella drew in a deep breath, nearly coughing with the relief of feeling her lungs expand. "What happened?"

Cristiano glanced up. Her gaze followed his and she gasped as she realized what she was seeing. A jagged piece of the roof was gone. And the wall. But that wasn't the most amazing thing. No, it was staring up at the rain-lashed sky through the branches of a tree that caused her insides to liquefy. The bulk of the tree had hit the bed, the branches splaying out crookedly in all directions.

Oh, God.

If he hadn't pulled her off there in time…

Only the mattress prevented the tree from falling to the floor and crushing them beneath the weight of the branches. As it was, they would have to crawl out from under the limbs that spread over them.

Antonella touched his face, flinching at the same time he did—and trying very hard to ignore the sizzle arcing through her at such simple skin on skin contact. "You are bleeding."

He swiped his fingers over his face, then probed upward, stopping just beneath his hairline. "It's not serious, just a scratch."

"It's a lot of blood."

"It's fine."

Antonella bit down on her lip to stop it trembling. Surely he would know if he were badly hurt. He'd said he'd served in the army, so he must have experience with this kind of thing. She had no choice but to trust that he did.

He lifted his shirt and wiped it across his face. "We'll have to crawl out of here. Can you manage it?"

"Yes."

He nodded once. "The going will be rough, but stay close."

Though Cristiano picked his way carefully, Antonella scraped her arms and legs more times than she could count. Shards of wood had splintered off from the main tree, and crumbled terracotta and stucco littered the area, making the process slow and painful.

She suppressed her cries of pain. It would do no good and she was determined to get out from under this tree before the storm did something worse. The wind swirled through the collapsed wall, whipping her wet hair into her face and making it hard to see anything in front of her. Rain pelted her, chilling her heated skin.

Fortunately, it was still light outside, because if it'd been dark, she didn't see how they could have made it. How would they know where to go? She'd stupidly left the master bedroom without a flashlight or a candle. She'd made her way to this bedroom in the meager light coming from the kitchen, the only room without shutters. Cristiano had a flashlight when he'd arrived, but he'd lost it, probably during the struggle with her.

It was all her fault.

They'd nearly died because of her, because of her wild emotions and stupid phobias.

Around her, the wood creaked ominously. Leaves rustled and the branches bit and scratched her tender skin. After what seemed like an hour, Cristiano turned back to look at her and she realized he'd made it through and was now holding the last of the branches up for her.

Antonella slipped beneath them and resisted the urge to collapse on the floor. Cristiano didn't give her the chance anyway. He stood and offered her a hand. When she took it, he pulled her to her feet. Pain shot through muscles cramped from crawling across the hard floor, but still she didn't cry out. She'd learned long ago not to show pain.

Pain equaled vulnerability.

And vulnerability to a man, in her experience, was like blood to a shark.

"Hold onto my shirt," he ordered. She obediently grabbed a handful, and then they were moving again. A few moments later, they reached the master bedroom. Compared to where they'd just been, it was so peaceful. The white sheets on the bed glowed in the candlelight, making the bed seem even larger than it was. Antonella wanted to collapse on it, fall asleep, and pray this was a nightmare and she would wake up in her room at home in Monteverde. Dante and Isabel would laugh when she told them at the breakfast table about her strange dream.

"Come into the bathroom," Cristiano said, grabbing the first aid kit he'd brought into the room earlier, "and we will clean these cuts."

For the first time, she noticed that he too was scraped and bloody. When he turned, she stifled a gasp. "Cristiano, your back!"

She hadn't been able to see him well when they were in the darkened hall, but his T-shirt was torn open over his shoulders and a gash spread across their width.

He glanced at her. "I know. You'll have to tend it for me."

In the bathroom, light from three skylights shafted down and lit the area well enough they didn't need a candle. Cristiano took a towel from a stack on a bamboo shelf and dipped it into the water in the sink. After he'd wrung it out, he handed it to her.

"Wipe away the blood and dirt," he said, then retrieved another towel for himself. He stripped out of his shirt while she worked on her arms and legs.

Several of the cuts welled up again and she spent more time pressing the towel hard against them in succession, trying to stop the bleeding. No cut was very deep, thankfully. She would certainly be bruised, though, where Cristiano had slammed her to the floor.

"When you've finished, spray some of this on," he said, pushing a bottle of antiseptic toward her. "I'm afraid it will sting, however."

"I've cut myself before. I'll survive a few stings."

When she sprayed the first cut, she thought she would scream. Sharp pain lanced through her, diminishing after a few moments. She repeated the process again and again, biting her lip and working quickly.

Cristiano was waiting with bandages. She had three cuts that needed taping up—one on her left arm and one on each knee. "I can do it," she said when he started to rip at the adhesive strip.

He was standing so close, his naked chest gleaming with sweat and fresh blood. His hair was damp with rain, and a smear of dirt crossed beneath his right eye. He'd wiped the blood from his face, but had missed the dirt. Even dirty and somewhat disheveled, he made her heart thud.

He didn't say anything, simply handed her the strip and let her do it herself. She bandaged her arm first, then her knees. When she looked up, Cristiano was watching her, an odd expression on his face.

Or not so odd, in fact. When she'd bent to bandage her knees, he'd been able to see straight down her dress as the wrap gaped open. In spite of the lingering pain of her cuts, heat slipped through her veins, caused a fine sheen of sweat to rise on her skin. Moments ago, she'd been chilled and sober.

Now, she marveled at the languid warmth creeping along her nerve endings and pooling in her deepest recesses.

Cristiano's eyes clouded for a moment. When he reached for her, she thought her heart would stop. Would he kiss her? Would she let him? *Should* she?

His fingers brushed her ear as he tucked a stray lock of hair behind it. A shiver ran down her body.

"Why did you think I would hit you, Antonella?" he said softly.

She stiffened. She knew he couldn't miss it, though she tried to shrug it off. She even forced a "how silly" laugh. But it sounded fake—and he knew it as well as she.

She didn't want him to see how close to the truth he was, how it rattled her to have him know something so deep and personal. How many times would she fall apart in front of this man she was supposed to hate?

"I'm sorry," she finally said. "I'm just a bit stressed. I over-reacted."

But Cristiano would not be stopped. "Did one of your lovers hit you? Is that why you thought I would do so?"

"Of course not!"

It was embarrassing to think of how she'd reacted, starting from the moment he'd told her about the bomb that had killed his wife. She was usually so in control of herself. But she'd let emotion get the better of her this time. She'd been shocked, hurt, and angered by the brutal death of his wife and by his accusation that she didn't love anyone but herself.

And then…

Antonella swallowed. Oh, God, she'd thought when he'd come in so angry and insistent that he was about to get violent with her. He'd been reaching for her, trying to tell her they needed to go, and she'd been so blindly out of control of her emotions that she'd panicked.

"You need to turn around and let me see your back," she said firmly. She couldn't bear the scrutiny of his gaze, the probing that threatened to unveil all her secrets if she were too weak to resist. And she was beginning to tire of always keeping up her guard, beginning to worry she would indeed spill too much if he continued with his sympathetic act.

Because he didn't care about her. She had to remind herself of that. It was most assuredly an act. His wife had died at Monteverdian hands—he had no reason to care one whit for any Monteverdian, no matter the circumstances of their current situation or the fact he'd saved her life when he'd yanked her from the bed and covered her body with his own.

Why had he done it? He could have left her there, could have stayed where he was and not come for her in the first place. But he had. And she hated the feelings of guilt and gratitude swarming through her because of it.

She prayed he wouldn't push her any further, wouldn't demand answers or keep probing. She didn't think she could take much more of it.

Silently, eyes hot in his tanned face, he handed her a fresh towel and turned. Antonella breathed a mental sigh of relief. It was short-lived, however, when she got a better look at his back. Blood dripped from a long, clean gash that went from one shoulder blade to the other. The skin of his back was stained red as blood and sweat mingled, and she hastily wiped it away.

She had to stand on tiptoe to see the cut better. Carefully, she pressed the towel along the edges, cleaning away any dirt and debris. Blood welled up as soon as she moved to the next section.

"I think it will need to be bandaged."

"I suspected that," he said with a sigh.

"Does it hurt?"

"Like hell," he replied, startling her. Not because it hurt, but because he admitted it.

"I'm sorry, Cristiano," she said softly.

"I've had worse, *Principessa.*"

She turned the bloody towel and continued cleaning the wound. "No, I mean for causing this."

"It is not your fault a tree fell."

"But if I'd stayed in the room with you—"

"It doesn't matter, Antonella. It happened. Let's deal with right now."

"Are you always so stoic?" She'd meant it as a gentle tease, yet he stiffened. A moment later, he relaxed again.

"I was not always, no."

She didn't ask what he meant. She didn't have to. He'd lost

his wife. It was a wound with the kind of pain that was worse than any other, she imagined. Did such a wound heal? Or did it scar forever? Would he ever love anyone again? Could he?

"I think I've just about got it now," she said, squeezing water over the wound for a final rinse and then mopping it up with a fresh towel. "I need to spray the antiseptic."

"Go ahead."

Antonella picked up the bottle and took a deep breath. "Are you ready?"

"Do it."

She sprayed the liquid over the wound, wincing as she did so. Cristiano didn't make a sound, though his fists clenched at his sides and his skin seemed to ripple from one long shudder.

"I think that'll do," she said, setting the bottle down again.

He dug in the first aid kit, came up with bandages, gauze and tape. "You'll need to wrap it tight."

She took the bandages from him. Another quick dab at the new blood, and then she placed the bandages over the wound and wrapped him with gauze. When it was done, she let out the breath she'd been holding.

He turned to her then. White gauze stretched across his chest, making him seem somehow more human and vulnerable than he had before. Where was the arrogant prince of last night? She had no doubt he was in there. No doubt she had to keep up her guard. Appearances were deceptive, were they not? She certainly knew that better than anyone.

"Are you okay?" he asked.

Antonella folded her arms over her chest. "Why wouldn't I be?"

He shrugged. "It's been a trying afternoon. And I'm fairly certain you are not accustomed to dressing wounds, *Principessa*."

She couldn't stop the bitter snort that escaped her. "You would be mistaken, then."

His brows drew together. "Do you volunteer in hospital?"

Antonella dropped her gaze. She started to tidy the items on the sink. "No. Forget I said it."

Now she felt even more inadequate. She'd never considered volunteering because she couldn't stand the pain and anguish in a hospital. Seeing others hurting made her hurt too. Yet another flaw, she supposed.

His hand closed over her wrist. She stilled, her heart pounding—and not from fear this time. He opened his hand, slid his fingers over hers. Then he trailed them up her arm.

"You are an interesting woman."

"I'm really not."

"But you are. You are a princess, a Romanelli, and though I believe you are quite spoiled, there is another side to you as well. A most puzzling side."

Antonella jerked free from his grip. "There is nothing puzzling about me, Cristiano. I am a spoiled princess, as you say. I've been around quite a bit, as you've repeatedly pointed out. I've seen things."

"In Milan or Rome perhaps? On the catwalk? Or maybe one of your Greek lovers dashed himself against the cliffs of Santorini when you threatened to leave him?"

"It was the Greek lover, of course," she replied, as flippantly as possible.

Before she knew what he was planning, he'd crowded her against the vanity. The granite pressed into her buttocks as she leaned back. Cristiano put a hand on either side of her, trapping her. The hard pressure of his body against hers was enough to make her weak with need.

Crazy.

"I find I have a need to know what it is that could drive a

man so insane," he said, his voice a deep purr in his chest. "Will you give me a taste, Antonella?"

"I-I...don't think...that..." She lost her power to speak as his head lowered. In spite of her inner voice telling her not to allow this under any circumstances, her eyes fluttered closed. His lips brushed hers. The contact jolted her so deeply that she gasped. He took the opening of her mouth as an invitation.

This time when his tongue slid along hers, she was prepared for it. And yet the feeling was every bit as disconcerting as last night on the yacht. She answered him with a stroke of her own.

Thrilled to the growl in his throat as he deepened the kiss.

She wasn't even aware of her arms moving, but suddenly she had them wrapped around his neck. She'd kissed men before, certainly, but never had she wanted *more* the way she wanted more of Cristiano. My God, he smelled delicious, all man and sweat and blood and spice. The combination was strangely arousing.

The kiss slid into the danger zone much faster than she could have ever expected. Cristiano's mouth was ravenous— and, shockingly, so was hers. Was it because they'd just survived death?

She wasn't certain. And she didn't seem to care. Cristiano's mouth was magical, his kiss the absolute center of her gravity at the moment. If she were to let go of him, would she float away into space?

It certainly felt possible.

Her arms tightened around his neck, her head tilting back so he could gain better access. A moan escaped her as his hands slid up her sides, his palms skimming along the outer curves of her breasts. Would he touch her? How would she react? Part of her was begging for him to touch her—and part was telling her that she had to stop this immediately.

She could not lose her virginity to the Monterossan Crown

Prince! It was unthinkable. The humiliation of giving herself to a man who hated her would be devastating.

Cristiano's palms slid back down her body. Then he gripped her hips and lifted her onto the vanity without breaking the kiss. His hands were hot and smooth on her knees as he parted them. Then he pulled her forward, her dress sliding up her thighs as her legs widened around him. When their bodies connected in that most intimate of places, the shudder that went through her was mirrored in him. The only thing separating them was a bit of cloth.

So many sensations careened through her: the hard ridge of his groin pushing against the softness of hers; the sparks of desire zinging into her nerve endings; the delicious pressure building inside her, demanding release.

And more.

The urge to *know* what happened next, to feel that glorious oneness that she'd heard so much about. To feel it with this man in particular.

The kiss hadn't stopped for even a moment. If anything, it intensified—

And then his hands were on her bare skin. His thumbs brushed the insides of her thighs, the elastic edge of her panties. Any second he would be beneath the thin barrier of silk and lace, his fingers touching her where no man had ever touched her before.

It scared her. The alarm bells clanging distantly in her head suddenly got far, far louder. This was going too far, too fast. No way could she have sex with this man.

And on a bathroom vanity? Did people even do that?

Oh, God, of course they did. She suddenly had an image burned into her head of Cristiano's nude body, of her naked and willing, him stepping between her legs like this, pushing into her…

She had to bite back a moan.

It would hurt the first time. She knew that. But after? Would it be as magical as she believed? As incredible as the novels she'd read? As amazing as she'd heard other women say?

She'd never wanted to find out.

Until now.

But it was out of the question. She had to stop him before it was too late.

"Cristiano, no," she gasped as his mouth left hers, as his lips trailed over her jaw and down her neck. His thumb slipped beneath her panties, brushed over the most private part of her.

"Please stop," she gasped again, gripping his wrists. Squeezing to get his attention.

And he stopped. Backed away, confusion clear on his handsome features.

"I can't," she said, knowing how inadequate it sounded but unable to explain. How could she ever say everything she would need to say in order to make him understand? "I can't."

Frustration crossed his face. And, surprisingly, resignation. How many men had tried to convince her, after one kiss, that she should allow them into her bed? None had ever simply given up.

But Cristiano backed away, removing the delicious pressure of his body. She wanted to weep with the loss. And yet she was relieved too. It was wrong to want him. And futile.

"Because I am Monterossan, of course."

Her throat was tight. "No, not because of that."

He raked a hand through his hair. She could still see the firm ridge of his arousal beneath his shorts. "Then why, Antonella? I know when a woman wants me. And you do. As much as I want you, God help me."

God help me.

Her heart ached as she hopped off the vanity and tugged her dress back down. "Maybe that is why, Cristiano."

"Because you want me, you will deny me?" Fury took the place of resignation.

"No, not because of that. Because you despise me—and you despise yourself for wanting me anyway."

His eyes glittered hot. "I am a man. I don't hate myself for wanting a beautiful woman."

She swallowed the lump in her throat. "Maybe not, but you hate *me*. I am Monteverdian—and Monteverde killed your wife."

Monteverde killed your wife.

Cristiano stared after her. As soon as she'd said it, she'd turned and hurried away. Left him standing here, contemplating her words.

The truth in them. Or nearly the truth, anyway. An enemy attack may have been the cause, but *he* had killed his wife. Killed her by marrying her. If he'd been honest with Julianne—about his feelings, his history and duty to the throne, the depth of conflict between Monteverde and Monterosso—would she have taken the risk?

It was a question he would never have the answer to. A question that both tormented him and drove him.

As if his thoughts weren't complicated enough, Antonella was adding to the burden. That she'd seen deeply enough into him to recognize his turmoil was not at all what he'd expected. *She* was not what he expected, if he were honest with himself. In spite of his best efforts to believe otherwise, his view of her was being forced into new parameters.

And he didn't like it.

Dio santo, his back still stung, he was in a constant state of arousal, and he was angry with himself. And with her.

She was getting under his skin in ways he didn't like. It was partly sexual, of course. She was beautiful, sexy, and with an edge of innocence he found absolutely riveting. How did she do it, as worldly as she was? It was no wonder men flocked to her.

He'd replayed the last hour in his head until he could no longer view it objectively. She'd been frightened of him when he'd tried to force her from the room. Frightened in ways he could only attribute to some trauma in her life.

But what? Who had hurt her?

Or was it an act? Was anyone truly capable of that level of deception?

If she was, she'd nearly gotten them both killed for it.

He simply didn't know what the truth was. And what he needed to do was shove all the doubt and thought and even the sexual attraction down deep where it wouldn't affect him. He didn't need to know Antonella, didn't need to understand why she'd looked so terrified, didn't need to know why she'd cried her eyes out in the taxi, or why she spoke to her brother every day and seemed surprised that he did not speak with his family as frequently.

None of that made her good. None of it excused her from the crimes of her family and their despotic grip on their nation. She was too intelligent to be a pawn.

Which meant she had to know what kind of things happened to those who'd dared oppose the Romanellis' rule. Journalists, engineers, scientists, teachers—those who'd spoken out during her father's reign were silenced. Some had fled to Monterosso and Montebianco. Others were thrown into Monteverdian jails, never to be heard from again.

Cristiano had no doubt the same thing was still happening. What incentive did King Dante have to allow his people their freedom? He'd deposed his own father, yet the military dictatorship continued. He'd made no moves to pull back his troops from the border, sent no peace overtures aside from agreeing to the ceasefire.

It would simply be more of the same if Cristiano failed in his mission here. More bombs, more guns, more tanks, more lives lost.

Cristiano threw the towels into a nearby hamper, put the supplies back into the first aid kit, and turned to go. A glimpse in the mirror stopped him. He looked cold, ruthless.

Exactly what he needed to be.

CHAPTER SEVEN

ANTONELLA dug a jersey dress from one of her suitcases. She frowned as she held up the jade-green garment. The fabric was soft and she knew she would be comfortable, but it was a little too fancy for a hurricane.

Unfortunately, it was the most casual thing she had. She went into the adjoining dressing room and locked the door before stripping out of her wet, torn dress. Tiny cuts lay across her pale skin like the tracks of birds' feet, remembrances of getting a little too up close and personal with Mother Nature.

After she slipped into the clean dress, she balled up the torn one and unlocked the door to the bedroom. She tossed the dress into her suitcase and dug out a comb. Her hair was a rat's nest of tangles. She'd had it pulled back in a ponytail, but that hadn't mattered in the gale force winds they'd endured while crawling from beneath that tree.

Oh, God.

Without volition, her hand stilled in the act of lifting the comb; that was when she realized she was shaking. She'd known it was close, but it wasn't until she'd had to clean and bandage Cristiano's back that she'd realized *how* close they'd come to dying.

It was a wonder they hadn't been impaled.

Surely she could be forgiven for losing herself in his kiss in the aftermath of such an event? Just as he could. She had to admit that if he'd been any other man, and she'd felt this kind of exhilaration when he touched her, she'd have thrown caution to the wind and let him do what he'd wanted.

Because there might not be a tomorrow.

Antonella shuddered. There *would* be a tomorrow. There would.

But if there wasn't?

She gave her head a little shake. It didn't matter. He was still Cristiano di Savaré, the Crown Prince of Monterosso. He was not, and never would be, her knight in shining armor. She wouldn't even be so attracted to him if they weren't stuck here together, if he weren't the absolute last man on the planet she should ever desire.

It was her perverse nature at work. The side of her that reveled in attracting trouble. Wasn't it her fault when her father got mad at her?

It's not your fault, Ella, Dante said after their father had sent them away without any food for being late to the dinner table once many years ago. But it had been her fault. She'd dawdled in the bath when she'd known she shouldn't. And she'd brought down her father's rage on them both. They'd been given nothing to eat for twenty-four hours.

Whenever she remembered an episode with her father, always there was something she'd done before he got violent. The last time was on the day he'd arrested the Crown Princess of Montebianco. Antonella had dared to tell him she had no intention of attending his event that night. She hadn't wanted to be humiliated when Nico Cavelli showed up with his new wife. And she hadn't wanted to see Lily Cavelli, to be forced to speak with her, especially not after she'd fallen apart in front of the woman in a Parisian salon only a couple of weeks before. Her father had been furious when Nico broke the engagement with her and married Lily; she'd mistakenly thought he would understand why she wouldn't want to be there.

But he'd backhanded her across the face, told her she would be present at the event and be dressed to kill. And then he'd threatened Bruno if she dared defy him. Bruno, her sweet little dog who loved her so purely.

She'd gone to the party, of course, in spite of the bruising on her cheek and under her eye.

And it had turned out to be one of the best things she'd ever done, because she'd gotten to know Lily. In the months that followed, she had become friends with the other princess. Aside from Dante, Lily Cavelli was her only friend in the world.

What she wouldn't give to speak with Lily right now! She should have talked Dante into going to Montebianco in the first place, and to hell with Vega Steel. But he was proud and stubborn and he wanted them to save their country with their own sweat and blood. He'd truly believed they could, and she'd believed because he'd wanted her to.

She heard the door to the bathroom open, but she didn't look up. Her heart rate bumped up a couple of degrees. She was beginning to get used to it, though she didn't like that she couldn't control her reaction to him.

In her periphery, she saw him cross to the bedroom door. He was still shirtless, the white gauze standing out in the darkened room like a beacon. He pulled the door open. A gust of wind blew into the room, and guttered the candle. Cristiano closed the door again and the candle flared back to life.

"Is it bad?" she asked, and then felt silly for doing so. Of course it was bad. There was a tree in the house, for heaven's sake.

"The storm is blowing a lot of rain our way. I think it will intensify over the next few hours." He retrieved another shirt from his bag, slipped it over his head.

"That door isn't going to hold, is it?" Antonella said.

"No, probably not."

"Shouldn't we go into the bathroom? Or the dressing room? At least it's another door between us and the storm."

He nodded. "*Si*. The dressing room is better. It is an interior room, and there are no skylights that could shatter in the night."

It didn't take long to gather their minimal supplies. Antonella tried not to think about how it would feel to be confined in such a small space with Cristiano for the next few hours. She would get through it, however. She simply had to remind herself it could be worse.

They could be impaled beneath that tree, for instance…

When she thought they had everything, Cristiano left the small room, returning with the blankets and pillows from the bed. Antonella accepted a pillow gratefully, putting it behind her and leaning back against the wall. She tucked her legs under her and bowed her head. Her eyes were heavy, but she couldn't succumb to sleep just yet. She was far too keyed up.

That kiss. It didn't matter how hard she tried to shove away the feelings, the images, she kept feeling his mouth on hers, his tongue stroking hers, his hands hard and smooth against her heated skin. She'd wanted him.

She still wanted him.

It was disconcerting as hell.

If she hadn't stopped him, where would they be now? Would they still be making love? Or would they be tangled together, sleeping?

She wished she'd never seen him naked, because it was simply too easy to imagine his body lying alongside hers. To imagine the smooth, tanned flesh, the ridges and knots of muscle, the flat, hard stomach that begged her to press her mouth against him, to explore him completely.

"What are you thinking, Antonella?"

Her head jerked up, her gaze colliding with his. Seeing her need mirrored there no longer surprised her.

"I was thinking how I wished I were at home in my own bed. With Bruno."

His gaze shuttered. "Bruno? This is one of your lovers?"

Antonella laughed. "Bruno is my dog. He is the light of my life and I miss him."

"You were thinking of your dog," he said, clearly not convinced. "This is not what I would have guessed."

"Then you don't know everything, do you?"

"Not everything, no. But the things I do know, I know quite well."

"And yet you can be mistaken, it seems." Except he hadn't been mistaken at all. But she wasn't about to admit it to him.

"What kind of dog?" he asked.

Antonella nearly breathed a sigh of relief. "Bruno is a Pomeranian. He's very cute."

Cristiano's mouth twisted, but she was relieved to see it was only mock disdain. "A girly dog. I should have known."

"And I suppose you have a great big pony of a dog, yes? The kind you can saddle up and let a child ride?"

Cristiano shifted his pillow and leaned back. "I have a cat, actually."

Antonella felt her jaw drop. She snapped it shut again. "A cat? Seriously?"

"Scarlett is quite probably bigger than your Bruno."

A giggle bubbled in her throat. "You have a cat named Scarlett?"

Now that was completely unexpected.

Cristiano answered her with a grin that made her heart turn over. "Scarlett O'Hara, because she is a self-centered Southern Belle." His smile faded by degrees. "She was my wife's. Julianne was from Georgia, and *Gone with the Wind* was her favorite movie."

"Oh." Antonella busied herself smoothing the fabric of her dress over her thigh. What was she supposed to say in reply? And why had he shared this now when he'd been so angry with her earlier? It forced her to see him as human, and she wasn't sure she liked that.

When she thought of him as a Monterossan, an enemy, she could fight her attraction to him. But when he was a man who'd lost his wife? A sexy man who seemed tender and caring? Who kept a cat named Scarlett O'Hara and knew she'd been named after the main character in his wife's favorite movie?

Madonna mia, it was too much.

"She's getting old now," he continued. "And she's very spoiled. I cannot seem to say no when she wants a treat."

The picture of this hard, ruthless man feeding a cat treats was mind-boggling. "She has you wrapped around her paw," she ventured.

"Yes."

His stoicism in the face of so much pain saddened her. She had to speak, even if he got angry with her. "I did not know about your wife," Antonella said, her heart tripping along faster now. "How she died, I mean. I know you may not believe me, but I wouldn't wish what happened upon anyone. I *am* sorry for your pain."

He closed his eyes. "Perhaps you are."

She waited for him to say something else. When he didn't, she prepared to lie down and try to get some sleep. The day was catching up with her and she just wanted to forget all the pain and trouble for a few hours. Maybe when she awoke, the storm would have abated and they could get out of here. It was a lot to hope, but hope was all she had left at the moment.

Her stomach rumbled loudly and she pressed her hand against her belly to muffle the sound.

Cristiano's eyes snapped open. "Why didn't you say you were hungry?"

"I didn't realize it until now." She truly hadn't. Besides, how was she supposed to be hungry when she'd been riding an emotional roller coaster since this morning? The emotion hadn't slowed, much less stopped. Hunger seemed minor in comparison.

Cristiano glanced at his watch. "It's been hours since breakfast. We need to eat, though we'll have to ration what we have." He handed her a box of crackers. "Open these while I uncork the wine."

"How long do you think we could be here?" she asked, homing in on his comment about rationing food.

"Hopefully not more than a day or two."

Antonella felt her breath catch. A day or two. Here. In this room. With Cristiano.

Heaven help her.

He finished uncorking the wine and poured them each a glass. Then he took a small knife and cut off a few slices of sausage. "Cheese?"

"I'll pass."

She watched Cristiano layer a neat dollop of the spray cheese over a slice of sausage on a cracker and pop it into his mouth. He didn't grimace, so perhaps it wasn't too bad after all.

They ate in silence, if you didn't count the wind and rain hammering the roof. Antonella sipped the wine, thankful that at least the island tycoon had a good supply, even if he had little else in the house. She wasn't much of a drinker, so it didn't take much to make her mellow.

And right now, she needed mellow.

"You never told me about Monteverde," Cristiano said a few minutes later. He sounded mildly interested, conversational—and yet there was an edge to him that hadn't been there a few moments ago. As if he'd made up his mind about something.

"There's not much to say. It sounds almost exactly like Monterosso."

"Yes, but Monterosso isn't on the edge of bankruptcy."

Antonella had to work not to choke on the swallow of wine she'd just taken. "I'm not sure where you hear these things," she replied carefully, "but we're moving forward now that Dante is King. Monteverde is fine."

"And did you support that? Dante deposing your father?"

"Yes," she said simply. What was the use in denying it? "My father was…unbalanced."

"I had heard of this. But what if it was simply an excuse for your brother to take the throne?"

"It wasn't." She picked up a cracker, nibbled a corner. "I was there, and I know what happened."

His eyes narrowed. "Interesting."

Anger began to uncoil itself in her belly at the tone of his voice. "Interesting? You have no idea, Cristiano. Do not presume to judge me or my brother for things you know nothing about."

"Then tell me."

She set the cracker down. She was no longer hungry, though whether it was because she'd had enough to eat or because of the sick feeling settling into the pit of her stomach over this conversation she couldn't say. "Why would I want to do that? It's my business, not yours."

"It could be my business."

She gaped at him. "How is this possible? You aren't Monteverdian, and you mean nothing to me—just as I mean nothing to you."

"I'm hurt," he said. "And after all we've been to each other."

Antonella set down her empty glass and leaned back again. "I don't want to play these games with you, Cristiano. I'm tired, I'm sore, and I just want to go home."

"But you were on a mission here. A mission you failed. Surely you aren't ready to give up so easily?"

Her heart thundered in her ears. Cristiano leaned over and poured more wine into her glass. She picked it up, only half aware of what she was doing. Sipped.

You failed.

"I'm sure you are mistaken. Yes, we wanted Vega Steel to invest in Monteverde." She shrugged. "We have a lot of ore, and it seemed quite natural. It would have been a good partnership. But there will be others."

"I think not," he said, one corner of his mouth curving in a knowing smirk.

Had she really felt sorry for him just a few minutes ago? It seemed impossible, incongruous with the man speaking to her now. This Cristiano elicited no sympathy in her soul.

"I think this was Monteverde's last chance," he continued.

The world threatened to cease spinning. "Last chance? You are deluded, *Your Highness*. This is only Monterossan wishful thinking."

"You can still save Monteverde, *Principessa*."

"You aren't listening to me. Monteverde doesn't need saving."

He leaned forward, eyes intense. "We both know it does. And I will give you a chance to do so."

Antonella ran her finger along the top of the glass to steady herself. Was he fishing for information? Or did he know the truth? She had to know if he was simply making wild guesses, or if he truly had a plan.

"*If* what you say were true—and I am not saying it is—what are you proposing? Will you tell Raúl you've changed your mind? That he should invest in Monteverde instead?"

"Monterosso will buy your ore."

In spite of the heat in the room, a chill washed over her. "We don't need to sell you our ore, Cristiano. We can sell it to anyone we choose."

"Except no one else wants it. Vega Steel will build in Monterosso, and while we have ore deposits of our own, yours are bigger. Between our mines, and the incentives I offered Raúl on behalf of the kingdom, Vega Steel can import materials from Europe or South America just as easily. We do not need your ore, but I am offering to buy it."

"You will build guns and tanks," she said.

He shook his head. "Vega Steel builds ships, Antonella. Ships, girders, and industrial products."

"They will build what you want them to build."

"It does not work that way. Raúl has contracts to fulfill. And Monterosso is not a dictatorship."

"Neither is Monteverde."

He frowned. "You know that is not true."

"My father is no longer King, Cristiano. Monteverde is not a dictatorship."

"Nevertheless." He poured more wine into his own glass. "You can save your country, Antonella. You have only to sell me the ore."

Her pulse was tripping into the danger zone. Her stomach threatened to upend everything she'd just put into it. She was trapped in this tiny room with him, and he was pressing her hard to admit truths she couldn't.

"The ore is not mine to sell, even if I were inclined to do so."

"The veins are on state property. Your brother is the King. It is in your ability to do this."

Was he insane? How did he expect her to talk Dante into such a thing, assuming she would ever agree it was for the best? It would be hard enough to convince him to seek help from Montebianco. But from Monterosso? Unthinkable. "I believe you are mistaken, Cristiano. Monteverde does not need to sell her ore to you."

His sneer was not encouraging. "Stop prevaricating, Antonella. We both know the truth. Monteverde is falling apart, and you have loans due that you cannot repay. Without this deal, you will fall into ruin."

"Then why not simply wait for it to happen? Monterosso can pick up the pieces," she said bitterly. "You will finally achieve all your aims."

"Stability," he said softly. "If Monteverde falls, there will be greater troubles in the region than you can imagine. Our enemies would pick Monteverde apart, and use the fragmentation to destabilize markets across the three nations. The war could spread with the chaos such events would inspire. I will not let this happen."

"If stability is so important, then why not loan us the money to make the payments?"

"What is in this for Monterosso? Nothing, except money we would never see repaid." He shook his head. "The ore, Antonella. It is the only way."

"What you say is impossible. Dante will never agree to it."

His gaze was sharp, as if he were scenting the air for weakness. She was very afraid he'd found it in her reaction. "He would if you convinced him it would work."

"It's impossible," she repeated. "Even if you are correct,

we cannot trust you. If we sold you the ore, we'd have no guarantees you wouldn't turn against us. You seek to claim Monteverde for your own."

His eyes glittered in the candlelight. A smile curled the corners of his mouth. Her breath caught. Why did he have to be so handsome? And so dangerous at the same time?

"You can trust me, Antonella. I would never turn against my own wife."

CHAPTER EIGHT

HER pretty pink mouth dropped open. Cristiano had to force himself not to lean forward and close it for her with a kiss.

"You cannot be serious!"

"Why not? It makes sense, does it not?" He leaned back against the wall and gave her a lazy look. He was so close to achieving his goals now. So close he could taste the triumph.

Her brows drew down as she studied him. It didn't surprise him she was suspicious. She was far stronger in spirit than he'd given her credit for when he'd first met her. Was it only yesterday? It seemed like weeks rather than hours.

Another woman would have fallen apart after nearly being crushed to death by a tree. But she'd endured, and she'd expertly taken care of his wound without a moment's hesitation or squeamishness. He was quickly learning not to be startled by anything she said or did.

"Which part makes sense, Cristiano?" she asked. "The part about selling you our ore, or the part where you think I could ever agree to marry you?"

He resisted the urge to scowl.

"Both. You sell us the ore to guarantee your loans, and I agree to marry you as a show of good faith. You and your brother cannot doubt my sincerity if I pledge to make you a di Savaré."

She snorted. Then she shook her head. "I could never do that to our people. They would see it as selling out to our enemies."

"Selling out? Or saving your country from a worse fate?"

"What is worse than subordination to Monterosso?"

"Ceasing to exist. Becoming a fragmented people owned and controlled by differing factions. Being consumed by civil war as your people turn against each other. No other nation will risk their assets to help you then."

Her grey eyes were huge in her face. A small cut over her cheekbone marred the perfection of her creamy skin. She seemed so young and vulnerable just now. Not at all the sophisticated and self-centered princess he'd counted on meeting when he'd flown to Canta Paradiso.

"You intend to gain control," she said. "I'm not quite sure how, but this is your aim."

"There is nothing in it for me." Guilt pricked him, and he shoved it down deep. He could not afford to feel remorse about this too. Lives would be saved. He had to focus on that fact. Once he paid Monteverde's creditors, it would establish who was in financial control to the world. Cristiano would make sure Monteverde was stripped of its weapons as part of the agreement. Without its ore, or the independent means to repay its loans, Monteverde would never again be sovereign.

Antonella tilted her chin up. Defiant to the end. "We still have options, Cristiano."

"Time is running out, *Principessa*. The loans are due in a week's time."

He could see the calculations taking place in her head. She was trying to decide if the storm would be finished by then, and how much time that would leave her to explore other options.

"Vega was your last hope, and he's gone. If you are thinking of approaching Montebianco, you should realize there is nothing they can do. They have agreed to sell Vega Steel their own mills, which will be run as a subsidiary. The incentive to do so was quite substantial, I understand."

Her expression hardened, but not before he glimpsed her despair. "So you have brought Montebianco along on your journey. I should have guessed as much."

"Perhaps you should have. It benefits both our nations to have Monteverde return to a free market system. There will be no more kidnapping of royal family members or attempts at blackmail."

Her eyes gleamed with unshed tears. "Blackmail," she snorted. "And what do you call this?"

"I will do whatever is necessary for an end to this madness. Monteverde cannot continue the way it has been. It's past time for change."

Antonella tossed her dark mane of hair. "Why are you even asking my opinion? My cooperation? Go to Dante and force him to agree with your scheme. See how far you get then."

Cristiano bit back a growl. "You will agree to do this, Antonella, or when the loans come due, I will make certain that Monteverde is destroyed forever."

Her breath caught. And then her brows drew down. Fury saturated her voice. "I thought you wanted stability. Or do you simply want revenge? Make up your mind, Cristiano."

He refused to acknowledge that she'd scored a hit. Yes, on some level he wanted to punish Monteverde for Julianne's death. Perhaps he would finally be free of this guilt once he had. But in punishing them, he would make the world better for them as well. Ironic. "Stability is preferable. But I will take my chances if you do not cooperate."

He knew she couldn't doubt he was serious; his tone was colder and more brutal than an Arctic winter. Part of him disliked being so remote and cruel. But a lasting peace was more important than her feelings. More important than his.

She remained very still, her grey eyes fixed on him—and then her chest heaved. Once, twice. A third time. He expected tears to flow at any moment. Prepared to deal with a tantrum.

She'd caught him off guard in the taxi. But not again. She would not manipulate him with her tears this time. He would not relent.

She wrenched her gaze away and pinched the bridge of her nose. Her chest continued to heave.

And then she looked at him once more. Speared him with a glare so full of hatred that he felt the icy blast down to his toes. Oddly, his admiration for her increased. And his desire.

"I will speak with Dante, but I cannot guarantee he will agree to any part of your plan. He may prefer annihilation to a devil's bargain with Monterosso."

Satisfaction settled over him like a warm blanket in winter. "I'm glad you see it my way."

"I don't, but you've given me no choice," she bit out. "Why didn't you save us both the trouble and simply tell me what you wanted hours ago?"

It was his turn to laugh in derision. "Would it have made any difference? Perhaps you would have fled into the storm instead of another room. We both know how that worked out." He shook his head. "No, I need you alive, Antonella, not running away like a spoiled child."

Her chin quivered, but still she did not cry. Amazing.

"Not all children who run are spoiled. Have you ever thought of that? Sometimes they run for self-preservation. Not that you would know anything about that, of course."

"I know about self-preservation, *Principessa*. I've sat in a bunker on the border while Monterverde lobbed shells at us. And I've rescued our soldiers from your torture chambers—"

"Stop," she hissed. "You chose to do those things. A child can't choose her parents."

Cristiano blinked. What the hell was she talking about? With a growl, she turned away from him and punched her pillow into a ball. Then she slid down onto her side and curled herself toward the wall.

He wanted to ask what she meant, wanted to probe and question until she spilled all her secrets to him.

But he would not. He'd gotten what he wanted. He was another step closer to victory now. Soon, Monterverde would belong to the di Savarés. It was what he'd wanted for the last four years, what he'd worked for.

So why wasn't he feeling triumphant? And why was he more interested in what she'd just said about children and their parents?

The scream that woke her was long and agonizing. So wrenching it made her throat hurt. Antonella bolted upright, but she couldn't see in the inky blackness surrounding her. It was hot, and darker than any night she'd ever experienced before.

Panic clawed at her, grabbed her around the throat; another scream pierced the blackness.

"Antonella!"

Hands settled on her, dragged her against a large, warm body. She fought, twisting and kicking, until something heavy settled over her legs, clamped her against the body that was so overwhelmingly strong and solid.

"Antonella," he hissed in her ear. "Wake up! You're safe here...you're safe."

Something in the voice pricked the bubble of her panic, deflated it—

And then she was crying, shaking, remembering.

She'd been dreaming. *Oh, God.*

"You're safe," he repeated, one hand stroking up her arm, back down again.

A trail of fire followed in his wake—and she just couldn't take the sensation right now. Not on top of the agony of her nightmare.

Her father, the lifeless gerbil, Bruno taking its place. Begging for her dog's life, her face bruised and bloody...

"It's okay, Cristiano," she forced out. "You can let me go. I'm fine."

She wasn't, but she couldn't let him keep touching her. He might want to soothe her, but he didn't care about her. He needed her as a pawn in his game, nothing more. He needed her alive and whole, but he didn't care if she was happy or sad or depressed or traumatized. Nothing mattered except his revenge.

Had she really agreed to marry him?

She hadn't actually said the words, but it was implicit in the bargain. Cristiano might intend to marry her in order to gain advantage, but she had no illusions about what a union between them would be like. There was no love, no hope. There was only suspicion and hate. It was a worse fate, in some respects, than a marriage to Raúl would have been.

"I'll light another candle," Cristiano said, his voice strangely disembodied as he let her go.

She took the opportunity to scoot away from him. "You don't have to. I'll be fine."

But she heard the flicker of a lighter a split second before she saw the flame. The metallic odor of sulfur and flint was followed by the waxy scent of a candle flaring. Cristiano's face was the first thing she saw.

Light spilled across his cheekbones, his nose, illuminated his eyes. Eyes fixed intently upon her.

"What were you dreaming about?" he asked.

She wrapped her arms around herself. "It's nothing I wish to share with you."

"Sometimes it helps," he said. "I know this from experience."

She shook her head, squeezing her eyes shut. "Stop pretending that you care, Cristiano. You don't, and I won't share the things that haunt me with you. It will only make it more difficult."

"How do you know it won't help to talk about it until you try?"

"If you're so into the idea, tell me about *your* life," she shot back. "Tell me what happened when your wife died."

She didn't miss the bleak look that crossed his face—and though she didn't wish to harm him, she wanted him to understand how it made her feel when he so casually suggested she talk about herself. Just because she hadn't lost someone she loved in so public and tragic a manner didn't mean she had less to grieve for than he did.

The tension in the small room was thick—and then he shrugged, and the tension dissipated.

"I wasn't myself," he said. "Not for a long time. I did things, said things. I hurt people, Antonella. I hurt them because I wouldn't let them help me."

She pictured him alone, raging, lashing out at everyone and everything. In spite of the heat, a shiver crept up her spine, made the hair on the back of her neck stand up.

"You must have loved her very much." She couldn't help but be curious. She wanted to know what it felt like to be loved so devotedly, how amazing it felt. She would never know that feeling, no matter what Lily had once said to her about the right man coming along when she least expected it.

There was no right man for her. She couldn't trust men, didn't believe any of them capable of loving her. She was damaged inside, emotionally, and that made her hard to love. Dante was the only man in the world who loved her, and that wasn't the same at all.

Cristiano flexed the fingers of one hand. That gesture might have made her recoil if he had been anyone else, but oddly enough she felt no sense of danger.

Suddenly, she felt as if she'd crossed a barrier she shouldn't. "I'm sorry, don't answer that. Forget I said anything."

He shrugged. "No, it's fine."

But he didn't say anything else.

Antonella cleared her throat. "How long were you together before…"

He seemed to understand what she meant without her finishing the question.

Once more, he shrugged. The movement was at odds with what he must be feeling, but perhaps it was his coping mechanism. She certainly knew about coping mechanisms.

"It was a whirlwind romance," he said. "We were together six months before we married. My father was not happy, you may imagine. She died a month later." He sighed. The sound was lonelier than she could have ever imagined a sigh could be. "There was nothing left of what had once been a vibrant, beautiful woman. Julianne's DNA was all we had left to identify her with. I buried a nearly empty casket."

She dropped her gaze to her clasped hands. He'd lost so much, had endured such pain. Because a Monteverdian bomb had exploded beneath a truck. It saddened her, pricked her with a guilt that she knew was not justified. She was Monteverdian, but she had not built the bomb. Nor did she believe it was the way to solve differences between nations.

Brutal, senseless violence.

Would he stop the violence? Was that why he'd pushed her

into agreeing to marry him? Did he truly believe a union between them could set an example for their countries?

Another thought occurred to her: why hadn't Dante done something to end the hostilities? She'd never considered it before. And it bothered her that she hadn't. But she'd trusted her brother implicitly, trusted that he knew what he was doing and that he was looking out for the best interests of Monteverde.

She still did.

And yet…

Why hadn't he done something, besides agree to a cease-fire, before now? If he had, would Cristiano be doing this? Would prosperity have followed on the heels of peace? Would she be here now, sheltering from the storm with an enemy prince and learning things about him that made her want to put her arms around him and hold him tight?

"My mother died when I was four," she said into the taut silence. "I know it's not the same thing, but her death left a hole that has never been filled. I empathize, Cristiano, even if I do not share the same experience."

His gaze sharpened. "And you still dream of this all these years later? Or is it something else that disturbs your sleep?"

She twisted her fingers into the blanket on her lap. She was tired and sad and—*Madonna mia*, did it matter if she told him? Would it really help? She wouldn't tell him everything—she could never share that with anyone—but could she at least give him a version of events that would make him understand her better? Was it worth the effort?

She took a deep breath, let it out again in a sigh. He'd just shared something very personal and devastating with her. She could give him something in return.

"My father grew violent after my mother's death. He became a stranger to Dante and me. We did our best to avoid him, but it wasn't always enough."

"He is the one who hit you." It wasn't a question, and she didn't look up. She simply nodded. He swore.

"He was ill," she explained. "I knew this. I should have been a better daughter—"

The swearing increased in volume and intensity, cutting her off mid-sentence. Hot fury crackled in the air between them.

Yet she wasn't afraid. Strangely, she wasn't frightened of his anger. It was…liberating to feel this way. She'd never experienced a man's fury without feeling the urge to flee.

Until now.

"That's ridiculous," he finally said, his voice roughened as if it had been scraped over sandpaper. "Children are not to blame for abuse. Not ever."

"No, but I knew I shouldn't do things to anger him. And I did them anyway sometimes."

"You were a child," he said fiercely. "It's not up to you to bear the responsibility for what happened. Your father is to blame, not you."

She believed him, and yet there was always that niggling doubt. If she'd tried harder, been better—

No. She had to stop thinking like that. Dante had always told her it was wrong. And now Cristiano. Why couldn't she accept that perhaps some things were out of her control? That she couldn't change the outcome simply by acting differently?

She swiped her fingers beneath her eyes, unsurprised to feel moisture. But at least they were controlled tears this time. She didn't feel on the verge of sobbing or falling apart.

"What time is it?" she asked, too emotionally drained to continue this line of conversation. And tired. She was still so tired.

He picked up the watch he'd removed and set aside. "Three in the morning."

No wonder her eyes felt so gritty. She shifted—and her body fought back with aches and pains she hadn't realized she possessed when she'd been struggling with Cristiano in her sleep.

He scraped a hand through his hair, yawned. Then he pushed to his feet. "I need to take the radio into another room to see if I can hear the weather report. The signal will be too degraded in here."

A sharp sense of loneliness stabbed her. Surprised her with its force. She didn't want him to leave her alone, and she didn't want to analyze why in any depth. It was a reaction based on their earlier experience with the tree. Had to be.

"I'm coming with you," she said, climbing to her feet. Pins and needles stabbed into her cramped muscles, made her long to sink back down again until they went away. But she wouldn't. When she made up her mind to do a thing, she did it.

His grin was almost tender. "I'll be back, Antonella. You don't have to come with me."

Her heart thumped. "How do you know? What if another tree falls, or if the roof rips off and you get sucked up by the wind?"

"You think you can stop this? Or do you wish to be sucked up with me?"

She crossed her arms. "Don't be silly. I don't like you that much."

His laughter surprised her.

"What?" she demanded when he didn't tell her what was so funny.

"You just admitted you like me."

"I did not!"

He reached for her hand, lifted it to his mouth and pressed a kiss against her skin. Shivers radiated along her nerve endings, through her bones. Rooted her to the spot and made her want so much more.

"You like me," he said. "You can't help yourself. Now, let's go see if we get swept away or if we can learn what the storm is up to." He handed her the candle. "Try not to let it go out. The wind will likely be strong in the house now."

Antonella followed on his heels, shielding the light with one hand. But her mind was working overtime as she concentrated on her task. The truth was more surprising than she'd have ever believed possible.

She did like him, in spite of everything. But the most frightening part of all? With the exception of her brother, she liked Cristiano di Savaré more than any man she'd ever known.

CHAPTER NINE

THE weather report, what they could hear of it, hadn't been good. The storm had strengthened, and the eye wall wasn't expected for another few hours. The rain and wind were torrential. She didn't need to see it to know. The sound was devastating. Though the master bedroom door hadn't blown open—likely because they'd shoved a dresser against it—she could feel the angry power on the other side.

For the first time, she began to think they might not live through this. She'd believed him thus far, believed his certainty and confidence in the face of danger, but her mind threw scenarios at her that had the two of them crushed beneath walls, washed out to sea, drowned, or even impaled by whirling storm debris.

Antonella shivered in spite of the heat in the dressing room. Across from her, Cristiano appeared to doze as he leaned back against the wall. She'd told him he could snuff the candle, but he'd said they had plenty.

She knew he did it for her. Did it so she wouldn't be scared or have another nightmare.

She couldn't tell him that simply falling asleep could bring another nightmare. It had been months since she'd felt too vulnerable to her wild emotions. Once her father had been put in prison, where he belonged, she'd slept better. Had fewer bad dreams. She'd become more confident in who she was, though she also knew it was merely a façade. Deep down, she was still the scared little girl cowering from her daddy's wrath.

Cristiano's eyes drifted open. She could tell the instant that he remembered where he was and who he was with. Awareness snapped into his gaze like a spark from tinder.

"You are not sleeping."

She shook her head. Her eyes felt as if someone had propped them open with toothpicks, yet she couldn't relax enough to sleep. Were they really about to die? There were so many things she'd never done, so many things she'd never said that she should have. Why had she never appreciated how precious each moment was? She'd spent so much time hiding, cowering, burying her feelings deep.

Even now. Shouldn't she be focused on living instead of worrying about dying?

"I can see the wheels turning, Antonella. What are you thinking?" His voice was deep and rough with sleep. Sexy. It stroked over her nerves like the lightest touch of a feather.

"Nothing important," she said. "I think quite a lot, actually. Sorry to say I'm not as empty-headed as you might have hoped."

His brows drew down as he studied her. "I never said you were empty-headed, *Principessa*. What's brought this on?"

How could he see past her veneer of scorn so quickly? How could he know in so few words there was something bothering her? It was simply another thing that made her feel more drawn to him than she should.

And more resentful.

"I'm just tired, Cristiano," she said on a sigh. "And I can't sleep."

"Did you lie down?"

"No."

"Maybe you should try that."

"It doesn't matter. It won't work." She chewed on her bottom lip. Cristiano's gaze dropped to her mouth.

Heat rolled in her stomach. Intense, overpowering. "Don't look at me like that," she managed.

"Like what?"

He was so incredibly male, so sexual. He aroused her senses simply by being in the same room. Looking like a bronze-muscled god.

"Like you want to kiss me."

His laughter was soft, but it sent a shiver through her nonetheless. "I want to do more than kiss you, Antonella. Much more."

She held up a hand. "I don't want to know. Please don't tell me."

"It seems like the perfect opportunity to pass some time. Don't we need to know if we suit?"

She blinked. "Suit?"

"Sexually."

The word sizzled into her brain. "I didn't realize I had to pass a test. Is this how you usually get women into bed? By asking them to take your test?"

She couldn't help the indignation that crept into her tone.

He grinned, disarming her once more. "I don't usually have to ask. And it's not a test; it's simply an experiment to see if we want more."

"More," she repeated.

"Of each other."

Her breath caught. Oh, yes, she could see wanting more. Wanting more of *him*. Never getting enough.

"That's ridiculous."

One eyebrow lifted. "Is it? Haven't you ever slept with a man who did nothing for you? Who didn't know his way around the territory, so to speak?"

Her breath strangled in her chest. "No."

"That's it? Just 'no'? How fortunate you have been, *cara*."

"I don't know what else you expect me to say." There was no way she could explain without also explaining she'd never slept with anyone in her life.

Something crashed against the wall outside. Antonella jumped, her heart in her throat as the aftershocks reverberated through the small dressing room. A second later, a gust of air blew under the door and the candle guttered. Cristiano grabbed a blanket and wedged it against the bottom edge, swearing. The candle flared to life again.

"The bedroom door has blown open, hasn't it?" she asked. The dresser must have sailed into the opposite wall. She could only spare a momentary pang for the Colonial French chest of drawers that had surely been smashed to a thousand bits by now.

"*Si.*"

But maybe it was worse. Maybe the wall had blown down. The grave look on his face made her heart pound. "Will we make it, Cristiano?"

His gaze swung toward her. He looked troubled. But his answer wasn't what she expected. "I believe we will, yes."

She'd thought he would try to prepare her for the worst—or tell her how silly she was, and of course it would be okay. She respected that he did neither, though she still thought the outlook was more critical than he let on. The storm was sweeping closer every moment. The power of it was staggering. Her hope was minimal.

"I wish I'd spoken with Dante," she said. Poor Dante. He would have to face the crisis alone now.

Cristiano reached for her, pulled her over and tucked her against his side. She did not resist. In this moment, it was nice to have companionship. To feel that someone cared. She knew he didn't, but at least he made her believe it for a moment.

"We'll make it, Antonella," he said, his breath hot against her ear. Did his lips touch her hair? She wasn't certain, and yet her body flamed at the thought.

Madonna mia, not now!

"You can't be sure," she said, drawing in a shaky breath. "But I won't break down, Cristiano. I know how to be strong in the face of danger. You can count on that."

"*Dio santo*," he breathed. "I'm sorry I ever thought you were shallow."

She tilted her head back to look up at him. In spite of everything that had happened between them, in spite of the anger and pain of being on opposite sides of a bloody war and the prospect of dying here together tonight, she smiled at him. Genuinely. He was more than she'd thought he was as well. Better. If they could come to this kind of understanding under these circumstances, what was possible for their people?

"No one is truly shallow, Cristiano. I believe everyone has a story. You only have to look deeply enough."

He slipped a hand into her hair, cupped her jaw, his thumb stroking her cheek. "What is your story, Antonella?"

"I've already told you more than I've told anyone else."

"I believe you have," he said. "But there's more, I'm certain."

She dropped her lashes, too startled by the intensity in his eyes to keep looking at him. He wanted her, she knew that. And she wanted him. But how could she when he wanted to steal her country?

She was weak, far too weak.

"A girl has to have *some* secrets."

His head dipped down and his lips touched hers. Softly, gently. There was no pressure, no urgency, just a sweet kiss that slayed her heart and left it wide open to him. Once more, she was aware of the fact she'd never felt this way with any other man. She'd never wanted one the way she wanted him.

Had never wanted to slip out of her clothes and feel her skin naked against his.

Had never wanted to open herself to him and feel the stunning beauty of his possession.

She wanted all this and more with Cristiano. What did it matter anymore? They would very probably not come out of this storm alive. He simply didn't want to tell her the truth of it.

This was her last chance to experience physical love between a man and a woman. It couldn't be wrong, not under these circumstances. She opened her mouth beneath his, touched her tongue to his bottom lip very delicately.

He responded with a groan. And then he kissed her again, more urgently this time. His mouth slanted over hers, his tongue demanding access. She willingly gave it to him.

So many feelings crashed through her.

Desire, of course.

Fear. Regret. Anticipation.

Of their own volition, her hands threaded into his hair, pulled him harder against her. His kiss shot up another notch, deepening, devouring.

She met him with equal intensity, shifting until she was practically on his lap, until the only thing supporting her was the strength of his arms around her. The kiss was spiraling out of control, but she didn't care. She only wanted more of this intoxicating feeling, this heat and fire that sizzled beneath her skin and made her think of things she'd never imagined.

Naked bodies entwined. Sweat and pleasure. Bliss.

But when he pressed her back against the carpet, panic assailed her. Part of her wanted to shove him away and run as fast as she could. She tried to withdraw into her shell, tried to view the events dispassionately from that deep, disconnected place within her—

And found she couldn't do it. Her usual refuge was denied. Anxiety spiked.

Something of her struggle must have communicated itself to Cristiano because he stopped kissing her, lifted his head to look down at her.

"What's wrong, Antonella?"

He sounded so tender, so concerned, and her heart careened wildly, skipping into her mental roadblocks, leaping against the constraints she placed. Her heart wanted to be free—and yet she knew it would never be free. Never free to love or be loved. Never free of the pain and anger of her past. Even if by some miracle they lived through this night, she would never be free.

Suddenly, it was very important to her that he understood she was innocent, that she'd never done this before. Because if they did move forward, if this was her first and last time, she wanted to know that the man she gave herself to believed in her.

"I—I don't know what to do."

He frowned. "You don't know whether or not to make love with me? It will be glorious, Antonella. Let yourself go—feel what we do to each other."

She closed her eyes, shook her head. "It's not that."

His fingers spread over her stomach, slid up to cup her breast. "Then what is it, *bellissima*?"

She dragged in a breath as his thumb brushed her nipple through the fabric. "I've never done this before," she blurted.

His thumb stilled its torturous track across her sensitive flesh. "Never done what?"

His voice was like a whip and she flinched away from it. He would never believe her. Never.

She pushed his hand away, struggled to move out from under the weight of his body where he half lay across her. "Forget it, Cristiano. It's just a bad idea. I'll sleep now."

He refused to let her go. His body pressed down on her, pinned her in place. And every wiggle of her hips against him only communicated to her the state of his interest in completing what she'd so foolishly begun.

"I don't want to forget it, Antonella. Explain to me why you do this. Why you are hot one minute and cold the next. Are you trying to punish me for wanting you? Do you enjoy these games? Because I grow weary of them."

She grew very still beneath him. Her eyes filled with angry tears as she looked up into his handsome, cold face. "I'm still a virgin," she forced out. "And I know you don't believe it, so please let me go."

"A virgin?" he repeated. "This is not possible."

There was a hint of self-doubt in his voice, but it did not cheer her.

She pushed at his chest. "Why not? Because you've *heard* about me, Cristiano? You know what they say about gossip, don't you?"

Cristiano watched the pink stain creep over her delicate features. Was she telling him the truth? Or was she so skilled at manipulation that she could stammer and call up a blush at will?

Dio santo.

He thought back to her reaction when he'd been naked, the way she'd seemed uncomfortable. The way she'd grown frightened earlier when he'd kissed her. She hadn't truly panicked until he'd hiked her dress up her thighs.

Looking into her expressive eyes now, seeing the hurt and anger and uncertainty there, he wanted to kick himself. They'd shared too much tonight to fall back on entrenched beliefs. He could no longer think of her as the shallow, greedy woman he had only yesterday.

She was innocent. In spite of everything, she was innocent.

She had every reason in the world to fear him, yet she'd trusted him enough to let him get close to her this way. She'd been trying to tell him she didn't know what she was supposed to do, not that she was uncertain of her decision.

The fact she'd chosen him, of all the men who had no doubt tried to bed her, staggered him. Humbled him. He did not deserve her trust.

"Antonella," he said. "I'm sorry."

Her eyes widened briefly. But then the cool princess was back. She was so good at hiding her feelings. Had she always been this way? The thought troubled him. She'd been abused and she'd learned to shield emotion as a way to cope. No one should ever experience what she had.

She looked away. "It's nothing. I am over it already. And I'm sorry to inconvenience you."

"Inconvenience me?" He laughed, a dry raspy sound. The irony of what he was about to do hurt more than he would have thought possible, given the circumstances. But he couldn't do this. He couldn't, in good conscience, accept the gift of her innocence when he never intended to marry her. When everything he did was for the sole purpose of gaining control of her nation and bending it to his will.

She deserved better. He threaded his fingers through hers, pressed a kiss to the back of her hand. Closed his eyes as her intoxicating scent stole to his nose. *Dio*, he should be nominated for sainthood after this.

"I cannot make love to you, Antonella."

* * *

Her heart was pounding so hard she thought she'd misheard him. But she hadn't. His face said it all. He had refused to make love to her.

Another man who'd rejected her, who'd seen that she was a damaged soul and refused to have anything more to do with her. Yes, he was the first man she'd ever wanted to make love with, but it was no different than her first fiancé driving off a cliff or her second rejecting her to marry another woman.

Men didn't want her. Not really. They wanted the idea of her, of her beauty and poise, but not *her.*

She closed her eyes, turned her head and pressed her cheek to the floor.

"Antonella," he said, his voice still raspy. Full of…regret? "You deserve better your first time. Better than a floor, better than a heated coupling brought on by desperation and the belief that our lives are in mortal danger. You deserve silk and roses, a man who cares for you—"

She snapped back to spear him with a glare. "You're forcing me to marry you. If not you, who? Who will make love to me the first time? You will allow me to choose a man, and then you will marry me regardless? I think not."

His brows drew together. He looked fierce. Possessive. Conflicted.

A little thrill shot through her.

"No. Of course I will be your first. But not here, not now."

Her breath caught. She'd heard the words, but this was the first time she truly registered them. "You really believe me?"

"I believe you."

In spite of her confusion and hurt, contentment washed over her. *He believed her.* "Thank you."

His index finger rubbed across her lower lip. Soft, sensual. Her body flamed in response.

"We will wait. We will do this right when it is time." He looked troubled, as if he knew there would not be another time. As if he knew they would die.

She refused to accept his decision. He believed her and he wanted her first time to be special. It was enough.

She caught his wrist, nipped his finger. Then she licked it. It was a far bolder move than she'd have ever imagined possible.

Desire flared in his eyes, scorching her. "Antonella," he grated.

"I want to do this. I want you."

His voice was strangled. "You are making a decision you would not otherwise make if not for the storm."

That he saw deeply enough into her to recognize that the hurricane affected her only made her desire him more. No man had ever known her so well. Not even Dante. How ironic that it was a Monterossan who seemed to understand her best.

"I know. But I don't want to die tonight without experiencing this."

"We aren't going to die, Antonella."

"You don't know that."

"I do. I promise you."

As if in defiance, a roar sounded outside the dressing room. Something exploded with a bang. A tattoo of rain beat harder on the roof, plinking the terracotta with a deafening staccato rhythm.

"Please, Cristiano. If tomorrow comes, we'll deal with it then."

"Antonella," he groaned, tilting his head back, eyes squeezed shut as if he were fighting himself. "You would regret it tomorrow, and you would hate me for it."

"You've forgotten that I already hate you," she said primly.

A smile curved one corner of his mouth. "*Dio*, yes. How could I have forgotten this?"

She lifted a shaky hand, threaded her fingers through his hair. His eyes glittered with heat and need. God, she loved the feel of his hair. Soft, silky. Black as a starless night.

"Kiss me, Cristiano. Pretend we're lying on silk sheets. Pretend that you care about me…"

CHAPTER TEN

SHE didn't think he would do it. He looked doubtful, even a bit bewildered at first. And then he lowered his head, brushed his lips across hers. Back and forth, so feather-light and sensual. She wanted to moan, wanted to clasp him to her and force him to kiss her the way he had earlier.

But she didn't. She waited, let him explore, let him do what he wanted.

"God help me," he said, "I cannot deny you. I should, but I cannot."

"I don't want you to."

"If you become scared," he whispered against her mouth, "or change your mind, tell me. Do not be afraid I will be angry. This is for you, Antonella. It should be everything you want. And if you don't want it, I will stop."

Her heart flooded with a warmth she hadn't felt before. A feeling of rightness and belonging. No matter what happened, this was the right moment with the right man.

"Thank you, Cristiano. Thank you for understanding."

His answer was another kiss, this time deeper and more powerful. Her nerves crackled beneath the sensual onslaught. Her body grew hot and damp. The soft spot between her thighs ached—absolutely ached with the anticipation and fear of what came next.

One hand trailed down her leg, slipped beneath her dress. His palm slid along her thigh, pulling her dress higher.

"Wait," she gasped.

When he pulled back and looked down at her, there was no anger in his expression. The relief she felt was tangible.

"Shouldn't we blow out the candle?"

His hand continued its path up her thigh. "Why would we want to do that, *cara mia*? I wish to see you."

She swallowed. "I…um…well…"

He kissed her softly. "Shh. You are beautiful, Antonella. Believe me, you are quite beautiful. My body aches, just looking at you like this."

He pushed himself upright, and she had a second of fear that he meant to stop, that she'd chased him away with her silliness about being nude with the lights on.

"I will strip for you, yes? If I am naked, perhaps you will have no objections about joining me."

Her pulse shot into a reckless rhythm. She could only watch as Cristiano smiled and pulled his shirt over his head. The white gauze contrasted with his dark skin, and she was shocked to realize that she wanted to press her mouth there, right there on that ridge of muscle below the bandage. She wanted to run her tongue over him as if he were an ice cream cone.

"I like the way you look at me, *cara*," he purred. And then he unsnapped his shorts and pushed them down his hips, along with his briefs. Only her second look at a man's penis up close and personal—and, oh, dear God, was she truly prepared for what was about to happen?

"Don't be frightened, Antonella," he said, dropping to the floor beside her again. He stretched out, propped himself on one elbow, and gently lifted her hand to his chest. "Touch me. Explore me if you wish. Or I will explore you if you are too shy."

She was shy—and yet she wanted to touch him. Her

fingers shook as she traced the hard ridges of his abdomen. His breath hissed inward when she dropped lower. Tentatively, she touched his erect penis.

"*Dio*," he breathed.

"Does it hurt?"

"Most definitely."

She jerked her hand away from the hot, velvety length of him. "I'm sorry."

"You can touch me again, *cara*. It hurts in the best way possible, believe me."

She tried again, growing bolder when he closed his eyes and didn't watch. His skin was soft, hot, and yet this part of him was so rigid. She wrapped her fingers around him. What had she expected it to feel like?

She wasn't certain. The intake of his breath brought her attention upward. He hadn't opened his eyes, and he didn't appear to be in pain—

She squeezed him. Was rewarded with a groan. A moment later, he'd pushed her back again, fused his mouth to hers and kissed her until she lost her mind. Then he lifted away again and started to pull her dress up.

"This needs to come off, Antonella."

She didn't protest. Instead, she sat up and helped him pull the jade material over her head. Her hair fell in long waves around her, helped to cover the lacy aqua bra she'd chosen this morning. Her panties, while not especially sexy in any way, at least matched the bra in style and color.

Cristiano's gaze devoured her. Oddly enough, she didn't feel shy about it. The way he looked at her made her feel sexy, beautiful. Special.

Had he looked at his wife this way?

No. She couldn't think like that, couldn't allow herself to go there. He'd loved his wife. This was just sex. She knew it, she'd chosen it, and she could deal with it.

He reached up and gently swept her hair back, revealing her breasts. When she would have covered herself, he gave her that sinfully sexy smile of his. "You are everything a man could want, *cara*. Never doubt that."

She wanted to weep at the tenderness of his comment, but he gave her no chance as he eased her back on the carpet once more.

"And now I wish to show you how beautiful this can be," he said, his mouth tracing kisses along her shoulder, up her neck, until he captured her lips once more.

Her body was hot and cold all at once, her nerves singing and snapping with every stroke of his tongue against hers. And then he broke the kiss, slid his gorgeous mouth down her body. When he pushed one of the lacy cups aside to bare her breast, her breath squeezed tight in her chest.

"So lovely," he murmured before his mouth closed over her nipple.

Antonella's back arched as her breath left her in a shocked gasp. An unbelievably pleasurable gasp. She'd never known it could feel so good. She clutched his shoulders, her hands kneading his skin as his tongue teased first one nipple and then the other. Before she realized what he was doing, he unsnapped her bra and shoved it up and out of the way.

Pressing her breasts together, he spent what seemed like hours—but was in reality only minutes—sucking each nipple into a hard peak. Again and again until she thought she would explode from the exquisite pleasure.

"Cristiano," she gasped. "Please!"

And then he was pressing kisses to her belly, sliding down her body until—

Once more, she couldn't breathe. Was he really about to do what she imagined? She wasn't stupid; she knew the kinds of things people did when making love, but she hadn't considered this would happen to her.

He traced his tongue along her panty line. When he pressed a kiss over the silk, she couldn't stop the groan that escaped her.

"You like this?" he asked, his voice rough around the edges.

"I feel so strange," she replied. "Like I'm about to dissolve into a million pieces."

His chuckle was completely masculine. Supremely satisfied.

"Let's fix that, *cara mia*."

When he slipped her panties down her thighs, she didn't protest. He pulled them from her legs and tossed them aside. And then he was pushing her thighs apart, kneeling between them…

The first touch of his tongue against her slick flesh made her cry out. But he didn't stop there. He continued the sweet torture, his lips and tongue doing things she'd never imagined. Vaguely, she recognized she was panting.

Recognized that some feeling was gathering inside her, pressing into a tight, hard knot, compressing again into something so concentrated—

When the knot exploded, she was shocked. Stunned. Gasping. Her back arched as waves of sensation rolled through her limbs, sizzling hot. After it was over, she felt drained of all energy. Exhausted. Ready to sleep for a million years.

Until Cristiano began the sweet torture again.

Twice more she gasped his name into the candlelit air, her body shivering and melting and reforming in the aftermath of stunning climaxes.

"Do you still wish to go forward?" he asked a few moments later.

She opened her eyes to look at him. At his handsome face, his concerned expression. She had the feeling that if she said no, he would stop right now.

And he'd be in agony, she was certain. Because she would have been, had she not reached her peak three times already.

"Show me more, Cristiano."

"Grazie a Dio," he said. "With pleasure."

He stretched out beside her, used his fingers to stoke her passions again. She was no longer surprised at how quickly he was able to push her toward completion.

Just when she was ready to come for a fourth time, he stopped and retrieved a condom from a pocket in his suitcase. She tried not to imagine why he carried condoms with him. And yet he *was* irresistible to women, as she'd heard more than once. No doubt it was wise to always be prepared. But it took a little of the joy out of it for her, knowing this wasn't his first time and wasn't in any way special to him.

It was just sex.

And isn't that what you wanted?

It was. She had no right to get upset because this was a casual encounter to him.

"Antonella," he said, the sexy timbre of his voice stroking into her razor-sharp senses. "You are thinking too hard again."

She blinked up at him. How did he always know? "It's nothing."

"Do you want to stop?"

"No," she replied honestly. She really didn't. Her body, while satisfied, was still keyed up in a very elemental way that she knew would never be fully appeased until he was inside her.

He leaned forward and kissed her again. "I was hoping you would say that. But if you change your mind…"

"I won't," she said, winding her arms around his neck to kiss him back.

Very quickly, the heat and need fanned higher until all she wanted was him. The past didn't matter. The future wasn't a guarantee. Now, right now, was all they had.

"Cristiano, please…" Her body was achy, ready. She reached between them, grasped that hot, hard part of him she wanted.

He gasped. "*Cara*, you will undo me before we begin—"

"Then we need to begin."

Cristiano swore, but he rolled the condom into place in a quick, smooth motion. And then he settled between her thighs. The weight of him, the hot press of his skin against hers, the blunt tip of his manhood sliding into her wet heat—

It was so much to process, and yet she didn't want to miss a single moment of it in her rush to fulfillment. She closed her eyes, tried to feel everything at once.

"This will probably hurt."

"I know," she breathed. "It's okay."

"Look at me."

She did. Cristiano smiled at her, and she felt as if she'd suddenly swallowed the sun whole. It was both a frightening and exhilarating feeling.

"Thank you for trusting me," he said. "I hope you will not regret this moment."

"Kiss me…"

He did, so gently her heart turned inside out. A second later, he pushed forward, sliding into her so far that she knew she was no longer a virgin. The pain was less than she'd expected, but startling enough that she cried out. He drank in her cry, then lifted himself on his elbows and gazed down at her.

"You are okay?"

She tilted her hips, getting used to the size and feel of him. Sensation blazed through her with each small movement.

"I—" She swallowed, tried again. "It's amazing, Cristiano. I had no idea."

His laugh was rusty. "*Dio santo*, it is a crime. And yet I am thankful I am the first."

Slowly, he retreated—and then he slid forward again, filling her more fully than before. Her scalp tingled. Her toes. Everywhere, there was heat. Heat and awareness that she'd never known existed.

Yet he was so careful she wanted to scream. Innately, she knew she could take more. Wanted more. Antonella tilted her hips up to meet him and Cristiano growled low in his throat. The sound thrilled her.

He began to move faster, though he took his time to do so. She knew he was being careful with her, trying to make sure he didn't hurt her, and her heart soared with the knowledge.

Soon, he anchored an arm behind her back, tilted her hips even higher—and Antonella gasped. How could it possibly get any better?

"Yes, Antonella," Cristiano purred, his voice like a sizzling brand in her psyche, "like that. Move like that. *Dio*, yes."

"Kiss me again," she pleaded, surprised at how badly she wanted him to, and at how fast she was spiraling toward a culmination that she sensed would be bigger than the last.

Cristiano's lips fused with hers, his tongue mingling with hers. He tasted of sweat and of her—earthy, sensual, and so overwhelmingly male she wondered how she'd ever thought she'd been kissed before he'd first kissed her.

Her climax hit her with a force that stole her breath away. She wrenched her mouth from Cristiano's, shocked at the speed and intensity with which her release hit her. She'd had warning the last time, a gathering of tension into a tighter and tighter knot—yet this time, the tension imploded in a flash, rocketing outward again in a blinding burst of sensation that had her crying his name in wonder and surprise.

"Antonella, *mia bellisima Principessa,*" he said between

wet kisses to her throat, her jaw, her lips. "You amaze me. So beautiful, so sensual."

She couldn't speak. It took too much effort just to breathe, to recover.

Cristiano's hips moved, and she realized he was still hard. Still ready. They weren't finished yet. The thought made her shiver in anticipation.

"Please," she whispered when she had the power of speech again. "Please…"

His gaze was raw—tormented?—but his eyes were suddenly hooded, as if he realized he'd shown too much emotion.

"Anything you desire, *cara mia*," he said. And then he began to move.

It didn't take long before she was gasping at the top of another peak. Cristiano's climax followed hard on the heels of her own as he gripped her hips and ground his body into her one last time.

Her name on his lips at the moment of his release was the sweetest thing she'd ever heard.

She'd thoroughly destroyed him. Cristiano lifted his head, once he had the energy, and gazed down at her. Her eyes were closed, and though a tear leaked from one corner, slipping down her silky skin into her hair, her half-smile of contentment told him she was not in pain.

He was still inside her, and more than anything he wanted to repeat what had just happened. But he couldn't. She *would* be sore, even if she was not at the moment.

Dio, a virgin. If his body didn't know the truth, his mind would insist it wasn't possible. She was hot and tight, and so naturally sensual it amazed him she'd not been with a man before.

Guilt snapped against the surface of his conscience. He'd had no right to take her like this. No matter she'd given herself willingly, she'd done so under false pretenses. Not only because she believed their lives in mortal danger, but also because she believed he truly meant to marry her.

It was wrong…

And yet nothing had ever felt so right—

No.

Guilt of a different kind speared him. Since the moment he'd awakened and looked into Antonella's frightened eyes earlier, he'd not thought of his dead wife once. He'd spent seven months with Julianne, married her, thought she was the woman he would fall in love with. How could he possibly forget her? She'd *died* because of him, because of who he was. Because he'd failed to protect her.

How could he lose himself so completely in the body of a Monteverdian princess?

He let his gaze slip down Antonella's form, over the perfect rounds of her breasts, the pink nipples so stiff and straight, the tiny waist, the apex of her thighs where he still joined his body to hers. A pleasurable shudder went through him.

He was just a man. How could any man look at this woman and not do as he'd done?

No excuse. He was a bad, bad man.

She must have felt him shudder because her eyes opened. She smiled and arched her back beneath him like a cat. One hand drifted up, smoothed over his jaw, tickled his ear before threading into his hair. "Thank you," she said.

Another pang of guilt stabbed into him. "For what, *cara mia*? The pleasure was all mine."

She yawned. "I could get very used to this."

"Yes, I imagine you could."

Her brows drew down at his tone, but she seemed to shrug it off easily enough. He cursed himself inwardly. What was wrong with him? She was a virgin—*was*—not a wanton woman with a whole platoon of lovers. She didn't deserve his sarcasm. She deserved far better. It wasn't fair to take his disgust with himself out on her.

"You deserved a bed," he told her. "Silk sheets, a bubble bath, champagne. You deserved to be treated like a princess."

She frowned. "In my experience, being a princess doesn't mean much when it comes to how I have been treated. I'm glad it happened this way."

Because he didn't want to think too deeply about her meaning, he focused on a red mark that marred her creamy skin where her neck and shoulder joined. And realized it hadn't been there earlier. "I have hurt you."

"What? No."

"Your skin. I'm sorry if I was too rough."

She touched the area in question. "It was nothing like that, Cristiano. Nothing at all." She yawned again, finished with a smile. "You were very patient with me."

Patient wasn't quite how he would have described it, but he was glad she thought so.

He rolled to the side, withdrawing from her body and gathering her against him. For tonight, he would hold her close. If they survived—and he expected they would—he would deal with his tangled feelings about this in the morning. He pulled the blanket over them, yawning.

"Can you sleep now?" he asked once he'd tucked it around her.

The only answer was a soft ladylike snore.

Antonella came awake slowly. Something was different. For one thing, her bed was hard. For another, there was someone else in it with her. Someone large and warm. A man.

Her eyes popped open. And then she remembered.

The dressing room was pitch-black, the candle having died

out presumably hours ago. She was lying on the carpeted floor, wedged up against Cristiano.

They were both naked.

Oh, God.

Images from a few hours ago played in her mind: Cristiano's body tangled with hers, his magnificence, his utter lack of shame in allowing her to explore him. His skill at knowing just what her body wanted and in delivering it so expertly.

The sound of his voice when he came.

She couldn't quite believe her own boldness at asking him to make love to her. She'd thought they would die, yet they were still alive. What was the storm doing now? She could hear the wind, but it didn't seem to be a deafening roar any longer.

She tried to ease away from Cristiano. Perhaps she could open the door a crack and peer out.

Muscles she hadn't known she possessed protested against the movement. Beside her, Cristiano stirred.

"Where are you going, Antonella?"

How did he wake so instantly? "I think the storm has lessened," she said.

He was silent for a long moment. "I believe you are right."

A second later, he was sliding away from her. The flick of a lighter, and then a candle flamed. Instinctively, she clutched the blanket to her breasts.

Cristiano's expression flooded her with heat. Sexy, sensual. Knowing. "I've seen it all, Antonella. It's too late."

"I know." But her cheeks heated anyway.

Cristiano pushed to his feet. His bronze body gleamed in the candlelight. He reminded her of a carved marble statue, he was so beautiful. He stepped to the door, then carefully slipped it open.

The candle flickered in the breeze coming from outside it.

"The wind seems to have lessened a bit, but I'll need to see if I can hear anything on the radio," he said as he closed the door and turned.

She dropped her gaze, afraid of what he might see in it if she kept looking at him. What was this hot, needy feeling uncoiling inside her? Desire, yes. But there was another emotion in the mix.

Companionship. She felt closer to this man than to any other person alive. It was a frightening feeling. Because he was still the enemy. In the cold light of day, he still wanted Monteverde's ore. And the fact she would give him anything, including her soul, if only he would make love to her again, terrified her.

How could she be so greedy? So self-centered?

"Antonella."

She looked up—because if she didn't, he would surely demand to know why. His eyes glittered diamond-hot.

"You are feeling regret?" he asked.

"No."

"Then what is wrong?"

How did he always, always know? It was unnerving.

She tossed her hair over her shoulder, tilted her chin up. "There is nothing wrong. I was simply hoping you would make love to me again."

He didn't say anything for a long moment. Her heart lodged in her throat. Perhaps she should have kept quiet, not been so bold—

"You will be the death of me," he said softly. "And I find I can think of no better way to die."

For the next two days they ate crackers, sausage and cheese from their meager stores, talked, made love, and listened to the weather. Antonella learned so many things about him in those two days—and she shared more of herself than she'd ever thought possible.

It was dangerous, and yet it felt right. They were isolated here, in their own little world, and each moment she kept wondering if it were their last, if the storm would finally claim them.

After their latest bout of lovemaking, her body ached—but in a pleasurable way. The soreness between her legs was simply a delicious reminder of all they'd done. She had no idea how many times he'd brought her to climax, but she was as worn out as if she'd run a marathon.

"I need to turn on the radio again," he murmured.

"Yes," she said as she collapsed against him.

He didn't move, however, and she was almost asleep in his arms when a noise buzzed in her ears. A different noise from the storm. A voice?

It sounded as if someone was shouting…

"Your Royal Highness! Prince Cristiano!"

Cristiano bolted upright. And then light flooded the dark dressing room, blinding her so that she had to throw an arm over her face.

"Your Royal Highness, praise God we've found you."

CHAPTER ELEVEN

EVERYTHING was different. From the moment when Cristiano's countryman had found them, her lover had been cool and businesslike. He'd ordered the man to wait for them outside, then assisted her from the dressing room after they'd thrown on their clothes and shoes. She'd wanted to go into the bathroom and freshen up, but he'd said it was too dangerous—in spite of the fact she'd been in there only hours ago.

Once they left the master bedroom area, Antonella realized the house was a worse disaster than she'd thought, with downed walls, a precariously teetering roof, and debris everywhere she looked. For the first time, she understood how much of a miracle it was that the room they'd sheltered in hadn't been destroyed as well.

Cristiano ushered her into the waiting Mercedes. One man stood at attention, holding the back door stiffly, while the one who'd come in to find them stowed their luggage in the trunk.

The wind blew her hair into her face. She brushed it back impatiently, her heart feeling heavier with each moment that passed. A light rain was falling now, nothing like the thunderous downpour of a couple of days ago. She turned back to look at the house again, but Cristiano's hand was firm at her back.

"*Per piacere, Principessa.*"

She climbed into the car, he joined her, and then they were moving down the drive, away from the house where she'd given herself to this man.

Where she'd fallen for him.

Her heart tumbled into her stomach and she turned her head away, fixed her gaze on the passing landscape. *Madonna mia*, how had it come to this? How had she fallen for the Crown Prince of Monterosso?

It had happened so quickly—too quickly. What would Lily say? She would love to talk to her friend right now. She felt like such a fool in some ways. She'd lost her virginity and fallen in love with the man she'd given it to. How clichéd and naïve was that?

She had no idea when it had happened, but somewhere along the journey from hostile enemies to unabashed lovers, she'd lost her heart. Cristiano was a man of deep feelings and strong convictions. He'd shown her that a man could be a partner rather than someone to be viewed with suspicion and fear. Everything about the last few days had been a revelation to her.

And what about him? What were his feelings?

She had no idea; it disturbed her that she couldn't get a feel for what Cristiano was thinking. She knew he didn't love her, but she thought that after everything they'd gone through he must care at least a little.

Yet he'd been so detached from the moment the man he called Marco had arrived. As if he hadn't been buried inside her only minutes before that, as if he hadn't groaned her name and told her she was beautiful to him.

As if they hadn't shared a thing.

The car whisked them across the storm-torn island to the airport. Cristiano spoke to Marco about the damage. It saddened her to hear that eight people had lost their lives, and yet it was a miracle that more had not. Canta Paradiso was beaten but not defeated. Fortunately, the island would recover. Cristiano instructed his man to call and pledge money for its repair when communications were back up. She wished she could do the same, but it was quite impossible.

Bitterness lay like acid in her stomach as she thought of why she'd originally come here, of all she'd failed to do. Cristiano had promised to rescue Monteverde, but at what price? She still didn't know, though she very much feared the possibilities.

When they reached the airport, the plane was fueled and ready, the cowling having been flown in and replaced just this morning while Marco had searched the island for his prince. Cristiano guided her up the gangway. His touch in the small of her back was light, impersonal. She tried not to dwell on how sad that made her feel.

A flight attendant welcomed them aboard, her smile never wavering though Antonella knew she must look as if she'd just climbed out of bed. She tilted her chin up and found her inner princess. She would need all her strength to get through the next few hours.

The next few days.

Cristiano ushered her to a plush burgundy club chair. "You must be starved. I will order something to eat for us."

"I'd like to clean up first."

"We will be airborne in a moment. You can do so then."

He turned away and went over to speak with the attendant, then returned and buckled himself into the seat beside her. She watched his strong, lean hands, hoping he would reach out and clasp her hand when he finished.

But he did not. He simply folded them on his abdomen and closed his eyes.

Dismissing her.

Antonella bit down on her lip. What the hell was wrong with her? She knew how to do this, knew how to withdraw and pretend not to feel.

Yet she couldn't do it. Not with him.

He'd broken something inside her, made it too hard to hide from him. She loved him, and she felt like an exposed nerve around him. Every feeling assailing her now was agony.

Why had she let him into her heart? Why hadn't she been stronger? When it mattered the most, she'd failed miserably.

As soon as they were airborne, the food arrived. The meal was simple, though far less simple than what they'd eaten over the last few days. She started to rise without taking a bite, but Cristiano touched her wrist.

"Eat first. It will help."

Nothing would help, but she didn't say it. Instead, she sat back down and picked at the plate of salad, the fresh crusty rolls, and the grilled chicken breast.

"Why aren't you eating?" Cristiano asked a few minutes later. His plate was already clean.

Antonella shrugged. "I'm not that hungry."

He put a finger under her chin, tilted her face up to look at him.

Ridiculous how her heart thundered. How her body ached for him, though they'd been intimate only that morning. Ridiculous.

His eyes were hooded, unreadable. Did he feel it too? Or had he already relegated the last few days to memory?

"You would prefer to shower, yes?"

"Yes."

Cristiano waved over one of the flight attendants. "Please show Her Highness to the washroom."

As she stood, he picked up a newspaper and opened it,

dismissing her from his thoughts as easily as he'd polished off the meal.

Once she was alone in the bedroom, she stripped out of her clothing and rummaged through her luggage until she found something suitable. The dress was badly wrinkled, so she rang for the flight attendant and asked if it could be pressed.

"But of course, *Principessa*," the woman said. Her expression was blank, her smile pasted on. Her voice contained a hint of ice that did not surprise Antonella. She was a Monteverdian amongst them, and though their prince didn't seem concerned, the rest of them were no doubt wondering what she was doing here.

In the bathroom, her reflection in the mirror brought her up short. *Oh, dear God.*

She looked like a woman who'd spent the better part of the last three days making love to a man. Her lips were red and swollen from his kisses. Her eyes were still slumberous. Her hair was wild and spilled down her back and over her shoulders in tangled waves. There were marks on her skin where Cristiano's growing beard had scraped her while they were entwined, and of course there were scrapes and scratches from the tree.

The tree's damage faded in comparison, however, to the overt sensuality of the woman staring back at her. Everyone who had seen her since the rescue knew what she'd been doing. What *they* had been doing.

She swallowed a hysterical laugh. Finally, her slutty reputation was true. How ironic.

The hot water on her naked skin felt unbelievably good. She stood under the spray for a long time, hoping her tension would drain away. It did not. Her emotions were winding tighter and tighter the more she thought about the last few days with Cristiano, and about what the future held once she reached Monteverde. How would she ever explain herself to Dante?

When the answer didn't come, she turned off the water and dried herself. The dress was hanging on a hook, the peach silk as smooth and shiny as a glassy lake. She slipped into her underwear, then took the garment from the hanger.

As soon as she put it on, she knew something was wrong. Instead of hugging her curves, the fabric fell away with the slightest pressure. Great gaps appeared along the seams as the dress dissolved into a tissue of scraps.

Whoever had ironed the dress had also sliced all the seams.

Cristiano looked up as she approached. The frown he gave her told her that she wasn't doing a very good job of hiding her emotions.

"Is something wrong, *Principessa*?"

"Not at all," she said smoothly. "Why do you ask?"

In her initial anger, she'd thought about showing him the dress, demanding to know who had destroyed the garment, but she'd realized it would do no good. Cristiano would not take her side against his people. And none of the flight crew would confess to the crime, she was certain.

It was a sign. A sign she didn't belong. And she would never belong here, even if Cristiano married her.

She just wanted it behind her. She wanted to get to Paris and get on the first flight back to Monteverde. The thought of being parted from Cristiano made her ache, but it was the only way she would ever gain any perspective. Perhaps it wasn't really love she felt. Perhaps it was gratitude…or even Stockholm syndrome, though Cristiano had hardly been her captor.

They'd sheltered together during a storm, and barriers that should have never been crossed had been obliterated.

She would pay for the breach. Was already paying for it. She smoothed the cotton of her sundress, the least wrinkled one she could find in her luggage, and sank into the chair across from Cristiano.

"How long before we reach Paris?" she asked.

Cristiano's gaze dropped to her knee, slid down her bare calf, back up to her face. So much heat in that look. So much promise. Her body couldn't help but respond. She uncrossed and recrossed her legs the other way.

Cristiano eyes smoldered. "Uncomfortable?"

"Not at all."

A flight attendant interrupted them, setting an espresso in front of Cristiano. "*Principessa?*" she asked, indicating the cup.

Antonella smiled so wide her cheeks hurt. "*Grazie*, but no." And give someone a chance to spit in it?

When she'd gone, Cristiano lifted the cup and took a sip. "Ah, *Dio*, I missed this."

"You haven't answered me," Antonella said. "Do you know how long it will take to reach Paris?"

"I do know, yes. But we aren't going to Paris. We're going to Monterosso."

If she hadn't already been sitting, she would have collapsed. "Monterosso? But you promised to take me to Paris."

"That was before."

"Before what, Cristiano? Before the storm? Before you blackmailed me into marrying you? Or before you spent the last three days having sex with me on the floor?"

He finished the coffee, the only hint of strain the tic over his cheekbone. "Before I decided it would be better not to allow you out of my sight. You might think, because of what has happened between us, that our bargain no longer applies. I assure you this is not true. I still expect you to work to deliver the mineral rights into my control."

"Work to deliver…?" Pain ricocheted through her. He didn't care about her at all. He only cared about the mines, and about defeating Monteverde. It was a business deal to him. Had always been a business deal. She knew it, and yet she'd allowed herself to begin to believe it might mean more. That *she* might mean more.

Stupid, stupid, stupid. Would she never learn? Had a lifetime of craving her father's love and approval not taught her anything?

Cristiano's gaze was as hard and cold as it had been the first night she'd met him. "You might be tempted to think sentimentality will deter me, now that we have been…close."

"Close?" She stifled a bitter laugh. Oh, my, the joke was on her, was it not? "Yes, very close. But not close enough, apparently."

"Did you expect you could change my mind by giving me your virginity, Antonella? I admit this did not cross my mind in the heat of the moment, but I see now it is a possibility."

"Go to hell," she spat. How could he possibly look back on that first time and think she'd been manipulating him? It was mind-boggling. Hurtful.

And yet she should have anticipated it. How had she ever thought they could put the difference of who they were behind them?

Something flared in his expression, but before she could read it he turned to look out the window. Silence lay between them for several moments. Then he turned back. "I apologize for that," he said. "But it changes nothing. You will convince your brother this is best for Monteverde. Because it *is* best, Antonella. It's the only way to survive."

She crossed her arms and looked away from him. Her throat ached with unshed tears. Oddly enough, his apology hurt worse than the accusation had. Without it, she could convince herself he was evil, rotten, and undeserving of her love. But he'd dashed that hope by reverting to the objective and fair Cristiano she knew lay beneath the cold exterior.

"It wasn't the only way we could survive," she said softly. "But it's the only way we have left, thanks to you."

Cristiano refused to feel remorse. Yes, he'd spent several pleasurable days in her company, but that was over now. He had a goal, and it was within his reach. He would not lose the war simply because he'd thrown a battle or two. He had to focus on the bigger picture.

He'd known, the minute Marco had found them in the villa, it was over; he could not, in good conscience, continue to be her lover.

He hated to hurt her, but she would get over it in time. He would keep her close until he was certain he had the mines, and Monteverde, and then he would send her home. He couldn't drag her through the pretence of an engagement for a moment longer than necessary. Not now.

Sending her away as soon as possible was the best he could do for her.

Even if she hadn't been Monteverdian, he could never marry her. She made him feel things that confused and angered him. Protectiveness, pleasure, companionship. Dangerous things.

Julianne's face loomed in the back of his mind, her soft voice asking why he'd let her go without him. He didn't have an answer. He'd never had one. All he had was the certainty he would end the violence and let her rest in peace.

He heard the click of the office door and looked up. He'd sent Antonella to call her brother. He had no need to be there, no need to listen in. He was certain of his position. Hovering over her would only add insult to injury.

She stood with her back to him, her head bent. His gaze slipped over the curve of her buttocks. Need was a hot current in his veins.

Dio santo, it had been a long few days. A pleasurable few days.

He pushed the insistent memories aside. They made him hard, made him long to take her into the bedroom and make love to her on the silk sheets he'd told her she deserved. She was so responsive to him, so eager and sensual. She may have been inexperienced only a few days ago, but she'd made up for it. When she'd kissed her way down his body and taken him in her mouth only this morning—

Antonella turned from the door and moved resolutely toward him. Her cool princess act was firmly in place, he noted.

She sank down opposite him and crossed her legs. This time, he worked very hard not to let his gaze fall to her bare skin, not to trace it up to where her skirt fell mid-thigh. Not to imagine what lay beneath that skirt.

Heaven. Paradise. Shangri-la.

"Your brother was glad to hear you were safe, yes?"

"He was very relieved." She studied a fingernail. Her hand trembled the slightest bit. Exhaustion, perhaps. Or nerves.

Cristiano frowned. He didn't like that she was tired or nervous. She deserved happiness. Her life, he knew now, had mostly been one of guilt and fear. And it bothered him a great deal that he'd added to her stress.

Yet he had no choice.

She blew out a breath and met his gaze. "Dante wishes to meet with you before he will agree to sell you the ore."

Cristiano masked his annoyance; it wasn't her fault. He'd expected reluctance, naturally, but he hadn't anticipated that the Monteverdian King would be quite so stubborn with time nearly spent. "What is the point? You have no options left.

Unless, perhaps, Dante doesn't mind losing his country to foreign control."

"Isn't that what you are offering us?" she snapped, her eyes flashing.

He ignored the accusation. "We are sister nations, Antonella. We understand each other more than a foreign power ever could."

There was something in her expression he couldn't read. Sorrow? Was she hiding something from him? But then it was gone, replaced by weary resignation.

"I don't believe we understand each other at all, Cristiano. If we did, then we wouldn't be at war."

"I'm going to end the war, *cara*."

Her expression said she pitied him. *Pitied him?*

She shook her head. "It will take more than one determined prince. I wonder if you understand your own people as well as you think you do."

Momentary shock rooted him in place. "What is that supposed to mean?"

"It means that old dislikes go deep. You can't change minds overnight. It's impossible."

He arched a brow. "We changed our minds about each other fairly quickly, did we not?"

She looked so distant in that moment. So fragile and beautiful. He wanted to drag her into his arms and kiss her until she blushed and moaned.

. *Dio.* He was losing his perspective. And he didn't like it one bit.

"We are only two people," she said. "And no, essentially I don't think anything has changed between us. We have been lovers, yes. But you do not care for me, do you, Cristiano?"

"I care," he said, surprised at the vehemence in his voice. He did care, the same as he cared for anyone he considered a friend. It was a huge admission for him, considering how he'd felt about her only a few days ago.

She wouldn't look at him. "Not enough, I am afraid. Not enough."

He grabbed her hand, squeezed. Her head snapped up. "Everything we shared was honest and real, Antonella. Never doubt that."

She seemed to hesitate, as if she were thinking about something. What she said next was not what he expected.

"I want more," she said softly. "Much more. I want love, Cristiano. I want you to feel what I feel."

He let her go, reared back against the seat.

Love. She loved him.

Why had he not anticipated this? She'd been a virgin, an innocent. She had a deep mistrust of men, and yet she'd given herself to *him*. He should have foreseen this complication. Should have been more ruthless with himself and refused to make her his lover.

Fire and ice mingled in his veins, warring with each other. Her words were seductive. He wanted to give in to the heat, wanted to feel that sense of connection with another human being.

But he couldn't do it. How could he possibly ever allow himself to fall in love with this woman? It would be a betrayal of Julianne, a betrayal of her memory and her sacrifice. If he couldn't love his wife the way she'd deserved, how could he ever love anyone?

Anger began to win the battle. Ice crystallized the flame. Shattered it. He'd made his decision years ago. He would not change his course now.

It was too late for him. Too late to ever go back.

"I can't give you more," he said coolly. "I lost the ability to do so when a Monteverdian bomb took my wife's life."

CHAPTER TWELVE

ANTONELLA didn't wake until the plane began its descent into the capital city of Sant'Angelo del Capitano. Sitting up in the recliner, she smoothed her hair. Cristiano sat a few feet away, studying a computer screen.

Her heart ached with love and pain. He didn't love her. Would never love her. He loved a dead woman.

Anxiety spiked in her empty stomach with each meter they dropped. She'd never been to Monterosso. So far as she could recall, she would be the first Romanelli in four generations to set foot on Monterossan soil.

The thought did not give her comfort. Nor did the hooded gazes sliced her way from the flight attendants. They did not want her here. Nor did she want to be here.

Cristiano tapped some keys, shut the computer. He'd showered and changed into a fresh suit, she noted. He seemed so remote, so handsome and regal. She tugged at her skirt, feeling like such a frump in her cotton dress. The silk would have been so much better, but she hadn't wanted to take the chance that another dress would be ruined if she'd asked for it to be pressed. She was so broke she couldn't afford to replace anything.

"You seem nervous," Cristiano said, glancing over at her as if he'd just realized she was there.

"Do I? How odd."

He smiled—and she wished he wouldn't. It only made her heart hurt worse.

"You have no need to fear, Antonella. You are under my protection. And Monterosso is quite civilized."

She wished she shared his confidence. But the remnants of peach silk stuffed into her suitcase were, to her, a symbol of the challenges between their nations. He might intend to end the war permanently, but she thought he would find resistance on both sides. Not because people wanted to fight, but because they didn't trust the other side to hold to their end of the bargain. She'd been naïve when they'd talked of this only a few days ago. But now?

Now she understood how deep the resentment could lie. It was disheartening.

The greeting awaiting Cristiano on the tarmac was nothing short of spectacular. An honor guard stood at attention on both sides of the red carpet as they descended the stairs. Antonella stayed behind him, hoping not to draw attention to herself. It was dark, but the floodlights at the airport lit the area like it was day. She slipped on her oversized sunglasses and kept her head down.

She wished she had Bruno in his leather Gucci bag. If he were here, she'd at least feel as if she had a friend in this hostile place.

As they passed the bank of journalists, flashes snapped and popped and reporters shouted questions. Cristiano turned and looped her arm into his. Then he waved to the reporters and kept walking. The flashes snapped more quickly than before as a collective murmur went through the crowd.

Seconds later, they'd reached the waiting Rolls-Royce and slipped inside. A uniformed chauffeur shut the door and climbed behind the wheel.

"You did that on purpose," she said as the car glided between throngs of well-wishers. Where had they found so many people to come to the airport this late in the evening? It was nearly ten, an hour when Monteverde had usually rolled up the sidewalks for the night. Not that her father hadn't been above staging scenes like the one just now. It made good front-page material for the paper.

Cristiano seemed puzzled. "Did what?"

"Drew attention to me." She knew she was a pawn in his game, but it hurt that he would treat her as such after all they'd shared. *Get used to it.*

He arched a brow. "I have returned with a Monteverdian princess. This is news. Far better to be seen on my arm than trailing behind me like a supplicant, yes?"

"They wouldn't have known, had you not told them."

His laugh was disbelieving. "Trust me, *cara mia*, you are very recognizable. It was only a matter of moments before they realized you were there. And I told no one you would be with me, though I cannot guarantee my staff did not."

Yes, she could well imagine the frenzy her presence on board his jet had created, even if she hadn't experienced the hostility first-hand. A Monteverdian princess was definitely news.

Antonella turned to look at the city. There was activity everywhere. Bars, cafés, and clubs lined the streets. People sat outdoors, sipping coffee or wine, while the streets were packed with cars and motorcycles. Horns occasionally sounded, as motorists got impatient with each other. Shouts and laughter and music mingled together as the Rolls slid past crowded sidewalks.

Sant'Angelo del Capitano was like Paris or Rome or Monte Carlo—always alive and vibrant. By contrast, Monteverde's capital was on its deathbed. Could Cristiano really save her country? Was his plan the key to returning her nation to vitality and prosperity?

She'd thought they *were* prosperous, but her father's downfall had revealed his excesses and how he'd really paid for his luxuries. Monteverde was broke and broken.

Fresh tears pricked the backs of her eyes, but she would not let them fall. She needed to focus, prepare for whatever happened next. "What is your intention now we are here?" she asked.

"As much as I can get away with, Antonella."

Her pulse skipped several beats. *Focus.* He wasn't talking about sex. Disappointment gnawed at her. How could that be?

She cleared her throat. "When will you meet with Dante?"

"As soon as it can be arranged."

"Will you take me with you?"

"Is it necessary?"

"No," she said honestly. "But I want to see him. We nearly died on Canta Paradiso. I want to see my family."

He inclined his head. "Very well."

She hadn't expected him to agree so easily, but she was thankful he had.

A few moments later, the Rolls pulled into a circular drive in front of a tall building. A doorman opened the car and Cristiano stepped out, turning and offering her his hand. This time, there were no photographers and she breathed a sigh of relief.

"Where are we?"

"Home," he said. And then he led her through the double doors and toward a bank of lifts. Another man in uniform greeted them warmly, then slid a card into the reader beside the lift. The doors glided open and Cristiano directed her inside.

"You do not live in the palace?" she said, blinking at her reflection in the spotless mirrored interior. Brass bars lined the lift, and there were no numbers displayed on the panel. It simply said, "Penthouse."

"I have rooms there, yes. But I prefer my privacy."

"It must be easier to bring women home too. Parents can be so style-cramping." She said it jokingly, but the look he gave her was serious.

"I have never brought a woman here, Antonella. I bought this place after."

After his wife died.

The lift came to a stop and the doors opened. She followed Cristiano into a spacious apartment decorated in masculine lines—sleek leather couches, modern artwork, glass and steel, cherry wood floors.

No, this definitely wasn't a woman's home. There wasn't a floral print or a soft line anywhere.

"Our luggage will arrive soon, but the staff won't be here until morning." He kept walking, shrugging out of his jacket and throwing it on a couch. Then he rolled one shoulder as if he were working out a kink.

A high-pitched meow came from one corner of the living area. Cristiano bent down as a fat grey cat lumbered over. A lump rose in Antonella's throat as he stroked the cat, talking to the animal softly while she purred and rubbed against him. This was a cat, not a child—and yet she could see how tender he would be with a baby.

As if he'd just remembered Antonella was there, he picked up the cat and stood. "This is Scarlett O'Hara, mistress of the manor."

"She's quite…large."

Cristiano scratched the cat's chin. "*Si*. I did tell you she was bigger than your Bruno."

For some reason, the fact he remembered about Bruno made her desperate to escape. She needed time, space. When Cristiano was near, he filled her senses. "Which is my room? I think I'd like to turn in."

"Your room? You do not wish to share with me?" He set the cat down again and she flicked her tail before turning and waddling into the kitchen.

"What is the point, Cristiano? You have said you cannot give me what I want."

He stalked over, looming into her personal space. His scent stole to her. If she closed her eyes and dozens of men paraded before her, she could still pick out Cristiano from his scent alone. His nearness set her on edge, made her body sing.

Made her body *want*. Oh, how she ached to slip his trousers open and take him in her hand before pushing him back and straddling him. She ached to do so, but she would not.

"You want me, Antonella. Just as I want you. And yet you are right." He ghosted a hand over her hair, backed away. "I cannot give you what you want, therefore it would be unfair of me to ask you for what *I* want."

Her throat ached. "Yes, quite unfair."

He stood so close, yet he made no move to touch her. His eyes were dark, troubled. And then he turned away.

"Come, I will show you to the guest room."

Cristiano took a sip of the whiskey he'd poured and watched the city lights. He sat on the couch in the living room, in the dark, Scarlett curled up beside him. He had no idea what time it was, though it was well after midnight. He'd tried to sleep, but couldn't. His bed felt too empty.

Antonella Romanelli loved him. *Dio santo.*

Many women had said those words to him over the years, and he'd had no trouble dismissing the sentiment. Typically, the women who'd said them hadn't meant the words so much as they'd wanted to be a princess and future queen. His mistresses soon learned he would not be persuaded by false sentiment.

I love you. Three simple words that hurt so much.

Julianne had meant them. And he knew without a doubt that Antonella meant them too. Or she thought she did anyway. Perhaps that was all it required to be true.

Each time he'd been inside her, his skin zinging with pleasure and a lust so strong it took everything he had not to come immediately, he'd begun to believe he *should* marry her. The physical side was amazing. Sex with Antonella was far more exciting than he'd thought possible. They could build a life on that sexual connection. There were certainly far less appealing things to base marriages on.

But each time it was over, he was torn. Guilt ate at him.

He should have known she would fall in love. She was innocent and sexy, so vibrant she made him crazy with need. He'd shown her physical pleasure, but he'd refused to consider that she might read more into it.

She deserved a man who could love her in return, not a man like him. He should have loved Julianne, and yet he hadn't. He'd cared for her very deeply, but if he'd loved her, he would have never let her go to the border without him.

He'd doomed her. He would not do that to another woman.

Beside him, Scarlett launched into a purr. He scratched behind her ears. She was the only real link he had left to Julianne. His wife's parents had died before they'd met, and her various other relatives hadn't been close to her. There was only this cat.

It was crazy to think it, but when the cat was gone, he would be alone. Shouldn't a man—a prince and future king— have a better outlook on life than this?

"Cristiano?"

He turned at the sound of her voice. It was scratchy with sleep, and she seemed to wobble where she stood, as if she was still so very tired.

"Why aren't you sleeping, Antonella?"

She shuffled over to the couch. "I can't sleep."

He held up his glass. "Do you want a drink?"

"No."

Scarlett stood and stretched, then clambered up onto the back of the couch and meowed at Antonella. She reached out and petted the cat's head. Scarlett began to purr again.

"She likes you," he said softly. "She usually ignores most people."

Antonella shrugged. "You said you've never brought a woman home, so…"

"I have a staff, *cara*. Some of them are women."

Scarlett meowed again. Antonella scooped her up and hugged her close, rubbing her face against the grey fur. The sight brought a lump to his throat. Julianne had done the same thing. The cat purred louder than before as Antonella came around and sat on the couch.

"I wanted to tell you something, Cristiano," she said, still hugging the cat. "It's important you know."

"Antonella, if this is about what you said—"

"It's not."

He could see her chin drop in the pale light coming from the city. She took a breath, then looked at him. She was in shadow, but he could feel her determination even if he could not see it in her expression.

"When we were on the plane, I asked for a dress to be pressed. Whoever did so split all the seams. The dress fell apart when I put it on." Before he could say a word, she rushed on, "Please understand that I'm not trying to place blame, and I don't want to hear you defend your crew against me. I just want you to know because I think it's important to understand where our peoples are coming from in relation to one another. I was under your protection, and yet someone

hated me enough to do this. And before you try to say anything, I know the garment wasn't damaged when I asked for
it to be pressed."

Anger spread through his veins like fire at the thought that
someone had done this to her. Someone in his employ. He
would find the culprit and force them to apologize—

Except he couldn't. What good what it do? It would only
make them resent her more. Resent Monteverdians more. He
wasn't the only person with deep and lingering resentments
toward Monteverde.

Dio, and he believed he would end this war?

Yes. He *would* end it.

"I'm sorry that happened, Antonella. I will replace the dress."

"It's not about the dress," she said. "It's about you. About
what you plan to do."

"If you are trying to talk me out of moving forward, you
are wasting your time."

"It's not that at all, Cristiano. I know you won't stop until
you've won. And while I understand your desire to end the
war and bring peace, I hope you won't allow your need to
punish us for Julianne's death to dictate what you do. Because
hatred and resentment go deep on both sides, don't they?
Many people have lost loved ones in the fighting. And de-
stroying us, while it might help you feel better for a short time,
won't really bring anyone back, will it?"

He couldn't speak for a long minute. Anger and despair
boiled together in his gut. "I am not a child, Antonella. I
know I can't bring anyone back from the dead. But perhaps
I can make sure the dead rest better, yes?"

She set the cat on the couch beside her. Scarlett climbed
up into Antonella's lap and curled into a ball. Her purr was
still as loud as ever. Cristiano tried to ignore it. Crazily, he
felt rejected all of a sudden. By a cat.

He was losing his mind.

"I need to know something," she said. "Is it your intention to destroy us? Or do you truly wish to end the war and help us find our footing again?"

He was on the edge of something, some feeling that threatened to swell inside him and make him burst. He could lie to her, but suddenly he had no wish to do so. She couldn't stop the inevitable, no matter what he told her at this point.

"I will do whatever it takes, Antonella. And I think Monteverde would be better served without the Romanellis in power. Dante may remain as a figurehead, but he will have no practical say in the day-to-day governing. That will be up to Monterosso."

Her breath rattled from her chest. "Yes, I thought as much. You never did intend to help; you only want to rule us." She bowed her head as if she were thinking of something. When she looked up, he could feel her anguish, even if he could not see it in the darkness. "And you never intended to marry me, did you?"

Pain arrowed into his heart, but he shoved it aside. He would not hide the truth from her now that he'd gone this far. It made no difference anyway. "No."

Gently, she picked Scarlett up and set her on the couch before standing. Her voice was soft, sad. "I feel sorry for you, Cristiano. You lost the woman you loved, yes—but would she want you to sacrifice your happiness to make up for what happened to her?"

"I did not love her, not the way she deserved," he lashed out. "Any sacrifice I have to make is my just penance. Julianne died because of me, because of who I am. I will not rest until there is peace between our nations."

She hugged herself, seemingly stunned into silence.

"Go to bed, Antonella. Save your love for someone who deserves it."

"I didn't know your wife," she said, "and I'm sorry she died, but you did not cause her death. Just as I didn't force my father to hit me."

"This is different," he growled.

"It's not." Her voice was tightly controlled, firm. "How can you not see that? You told me I was wrong to believe I could have changed my father's actions, that my behavior had nothing to do with his. And yet you think you somehow forced Julianne into that convoy? That you set the bomb and waited until she was on top of it?"

"Antonella—"

"No. You're wrong, Cristiano. I don't care what you think, but you're wrong. It's not your fault." She sucked in a ragged breath and he realized how close to tears she was.

He also knew she would not give in to them.

"I could have stopped her from going." Should have stopped her.

"You aren't omniscient. None of us are. I should have stayed home instead of going to Canta Paradiso. I would have missed the storm. And I could still call my heart my own."

He didn't say anything as she whirled and strode away. What good would it do? Scarlett jumped off the couch and followed her at a trot. A door snapped shut, then opened again when the cat meowed.

When it shut again, he was truly alone. Even the cat had forsaken him.

CHAPTER THIRTEEN

IN THE morning when Antonella awoke, with the cat curled up beside her, she felt more lonely and angry than she ever had in her life. She was in love with a man who was enslaved to a memory.

A man who'd lied to her. Knowing he'd never intended to marry her hurt more than it should, considering she'd been so angry when he'd forced her into the agreement in the first place. He'd only done so as a method of ensuring she would believe he intended to help Monteverde.

And she supposed he would help, in a way, though he also intended to destroy Monteverde's independence. Was it wrong of her to think that maybe blending the two nations might indeed work toward eroding hostility and misunderstanding? Cristiano was not so stupid as to depose Dante outright, which meant he was actually thinking about more than revenge.

Yet it did not give her comfort.

It was up to Dante now, though she believed he would not fight. It was too late. Without an eleventh hour rescue from a generous benefactor, Cristiano's money was their last resort. It was either that or allow Monteverde to be carved up by squabbling creditors, which could prolong her country's suffering. She did not believe Dante wanted that any more than she did.

After she dressed, she emerged from the room to find Cristiano waiting at the breakfast table. A uniformed woman served coffee and pastries to him while he read the morning paper. Antonella joined him, though her stomach refused to hold a bite of food.

"We will fly to Montebianco in two hours," he said without preamble. "Your brother will meet us there."

He didn't speak to her again. And though she ached for him, ached to reach out and simply ghost her fingers along his skin, as if the touch could last her a lifetime, she did nothing of the sort.

It was a long, lonely ride back to the airport, sitting beside him and not speaking. Feeling his presence in every nerve and cell of her body and being unable to act on it.

Far better to go home and try to build her life without him than be so close to him and unable to reach him.

But, if that was true, why did it make her ache so much?

Men. They were as cruel and untrustworthy as she'd always believed, though not just in the ways she'd always thought. No, some of them were cruel in what they withheld, untrustworthy in what they refused to feel. If only there was a way to know this at the beginning, a way to see inside a person and realize they could never be what you needed. That if they couldn't be honest with themselves, they could never be so with you.

He blamed himself for his wife's death, and he was angry and bitter because of it. She ached for him, but she could never change him. He had to change himself.

The only bright spot about going to Montebianco, aside from being reunited with Dante, was seeing Lily again. She was not on the helipad when they landed, but when they were shown into the palace, a very pregnant Lily rushed—if it could indeed be called rushing—to clasp Antonella in an embrace.

When she stepped back, her gaze widened. "Ella, you've changed!"

Antonella glanced over at Cristiano. He was deep in conversation with Nico Cavelli, the Crown Prince of Montebianco.

"It's nothing, I assure you. It's been a trying few days sheltering from the storm, that is all."

"I heard about that. My goodness, how frightening that must have been. Just you and Cristiano, hmm?" Her eyes gleamed. "Perhaps this explains why you look different to me. What did you and the handsome prince do all alone, Ella?"

Antonella rolled her eyes as if the question was beyond silly. Because, though she'd desperately wanted to talk to her friend just yesterday, she couldn't speak about it right now. She felt too raw, too exposed. "We did nothing except try to stay alive. Your imagination has run away with you. No doubt because you are pregnant."

Lily sighed, resting her hands over her belly. "Another month to go, yet I feel like I could pop at any moment."

Nico must have had some sixth sense about his wife because the moment the words left her lips, he was there, ushering her to a seat, helping her down into it, and offering to bring her a cool drink. Antonella looked away. She couldn't stand to watch a couple in love right at this moment, couldn't bear to see how Nico looked at his wife, or the way her face glowed with unconditional love as he pressed a kiss to her lips.

She didn't mean to do it, but she glanced at Cristiano. He was watching her, his gaze locking with hers for a long moment as her heart thundered in her ears. But then he turned and left her feeling bereft at the loss of contact. She'd hoped he would see why he was wrong, but she knew he would not.

There would be no unconditional love for her. She had always known she wasn't meant to find happiness, so why start crying over it now?

Soon, her brother arrived. Antonella ran into his outstretched arms and hugged him tight. He held her for a long moment, squeezing her to him. Ridiculously, she started to cry.

"What is wrong, Ella?" he said. "You are safe, and I am very happy to have you so."

"I failed us, Dante," she whispered. "I failed."

"No," he said firmly. "It is I who have failed. Whatever happens now, you will not blame yourself."

"I should have tried harder—"

"Ella," he said, kissing her brow, "sweet little Ella. Always you blame yourself, and always you are wrong. Let it go, *la mia sorellina*."

He gave her another squeeze, then set her gently away from him. Cristiano stood nearby, his expression blank. Antonella couldn't bear to look at him a moment longer. She turned and walked out onto the nearest terrazzo. She needed a moment to breathe, to get her head on straight again.

But when she'd collected her thoughts and returned to the room, the three men had gone.

Lily frowned at her, determination set in her expression like a sculpture carved from marble. "I think we need to talk, Antonella."

Antonella let out a long sigh. "*Si*, I believe you are right."

The men were closeted together for several hours. Antonella chafed at not knowing what was going on. Anger had begun as a little teasing dance in her heart, then swirled up into a lashing storm that brewed inside her with the force of the hurricane she'd just survived.

Anger at her father for so many things: bankrupting Monteverde, causing this crisis, hurting her and Dante, refusing to see her as anything other than a beautiful object to be bartered in the service of her country.

When this was over, no matter what happened, she was doing a few things differently.

For one thing, she was going to look into taking a university course to learn something useful. Let someone else pour tea and smile delightedly while engaging in idle chit-chat with the spouses of foreign dignitaries. She was capable of so much more, and she longed to prove it.

She was angry with her brother for not acting more decisively sooner, for not making overtures to Monterosso, and for refusing to listen to her advice when she'd given it.

She was also angry with Cristiano. His inability to let go of his wife's death, his need for revenge, and his refusal to accept her love for the gift it was infuriated her. Because, yes, her love *was* worthwhile. *She* was worthwhile.

And she refused to let anyone make her feel inferior ever again. Talking with Lily helped to clarify her feelings. Lily didn't tell her what to do, didn't judge her or offer suggestions— she merely asked questions about what had happened and how those events made Antonella feel.

When she had to consider, *really consider,* what her feelings were about everything, she'd grown angry.

How *dare* he dismiss her so easily? How dare he accept her innocence, ask for her trust, and dig into her personal life, her deep pain and anguish, without ever intending to care for her or to follow through on his declaration they would marry?

She was blazing angry the more she thought about it. He'd

used her, in more ways than one. Yes, he'd saved her life, and she was grateful, but it didn't excuse his deception—a deception that had begun long before they'd sheltered from the storm.

When Lily excused herself, saying she had to speak with the cook about dinner, Antonella remained on the small terrace off Lily's sitting room, sipping a glass of sweet iced tea—a delicacy from Lily's native southern United States—and thinking.

"Antonella."

Her heart leapt into her throat at the deep, sexy timbre of his voice. She set the tea down and gazed up at him as coolly as she could muster. Lily must have told him where to find her. Bless her meddling friend, but the last thing Antonella needed was to talk to him right now.

"How did it go, Cristiano? Are you the conquering hero now? Should I bow and call you master?"

His expression was unreadable. Blank and impersonal. Her fury whipped higher.

"That is hardly necessary," he said. "Dante has agreed to sell me the ore, and I have agreed to guarantee your loans in exchange. It is the best possible scenario for us all."

"Oh, yes, quite the best. How did he take it when you informed him he would only be a figurehead?"

"Monterosso will send government advisors to assist with the recovery. Dante is still King."

"For how long, I wonder?" she said softly. It meant nothing, and she refused to read more into it. The advisors would run the country. Surely Dante knew it as well.

Cristiano scraped a hand through his hair as he threw himself into the chair Lily had vacated. "I don't want it to end like this between us, Antonella."

She crossed her arms to keep from wrapping her hands

around his throat. Her entire body trembled with emotion. Anger, pain, betrayal.

Love.

"End like what, Cristiano? End with you triumphant? Riding off into the sunset with your shiny new toy and your freedom from messy entanglements?"

"You are angry."

She snorted. "What gave it away, I wonder?"

A flash of answering rage crossed his handsome face. "We shared too much to be enemies now, don't you think?"

"I think we were always enemies, Your Royal Highness. I made the mistake of forgetting for a while. I won't do so again, I assure you."

His smile was weary, resigned. "It wouldn't have worked out between us, *cara*. Even if we were to marry, and our people accepted it, you would hate me before the end. I have told you I cannot give you what you desire. As much as I do care for you, and as much as I want you in my bed, it is unfair of me to claim you. You deserve to be loved, Antonella. Loved in a way I can never give you."

A tear spilled down her cheek and she dashed it away. "I'm angry, so please don't think I cry because you have broken my heart," she bit out. "And please stop making excuses for your behavior by telling me what I deserve. I *know* what I deserve, Cristiano."

"I'm not making excuses. I am simply informing you of the facts."

"Yes, well, I am aware of the facts. And I am also aware that if you begged me to marry you right this moment, I would refuse. Because what I deserve is a man who believes in me. Anyone can claim to love another person. Believing in them no matter what, trusting yourself to them—that's the hard part, isn't it?"

"I believe you are capable of anything you set your mind to, Antonella. You will have a good life without me in it. And you will find that man you seek."

She turned her head. She didn't want him to see the despair, the hole his absence would leave. Because no matter what she said, no matter how brave she was or how right her convictions, *he* was the man she loved.

And it would take a very long time to get over him.

"You may leave now, Cristiano. I don't think we have anything left to say to one another."

He didn't move for a long minute. She prayed he would not reach out and touch her, wouldn't try to give her a farewell kiss or shake her hand or something equally devastating.

Because she would crumble into a million bits and blow away in the breeze if he did so. She felt that fragile at the moment. Fragile as spun glass.

It wasn't a good feeling. It was, in fact, quite possibly the lowest feeling she'd ever had. And that was pretty amazing, considering the things that had happened to her during her life.

He didn't reach for her. He stood and strode away without a word. She sat there, quite numb, listening to the wind bringing her snippets of laughter and chatter from somewhere below the terrace long after his footsteps had faded away.

Cristiano was in a foul mood when he boarded the helicopter that would take him home.

Home.

He had no wish to return to his apartment. It had been his refuge after Julianne died, the place he retreated to where he wasn't haunted by memories of her in bed with him or laughing at him over the breakfast table.

It had been safe—until he'd brought Antonella into it. She

had only spent one night there. One morning at the table. Add in one late night talk with Julianne's fickle cat curled up on Antonella's lap as if she were the new mistress of the manor, and his peace was ruined.

Or had it been ruined before that?

The moment she'd given herself to him? The moment he'd dragged her from the bed and rolled her beneath him to prevent the tree from crushing her? The moment she'd sobbed in the taxi as if her heart were shattering? Or was it the moment she'd turned from her door on the deck of the yacht?

He pressed his fingers on either side of his temples, hoping to rub out the headache that was fast settling in. It was strain, nothing more. The strain of the last week—all the planning, the travel, the storm, the talk just now with Dante Romanelli.

Surprisingly, he liked the Monteverdian King. He sensed no deceit in the other man, no sinister intention. King Dante was younger than he was by a couple of years, and yet the other man seemed much older and more worn out. The stress of governing under the circumstances he had for the last six months had taken a toll.

Cristiano found himself thinking, while talking with the King, that this man could be the right person to guide Monteverde forward after all. But he'd already put his plan in motion; it was too late to modify it, nor would he do so based on a first impression. Once Dante had signed the agreements Cristiano had his lawyers draw up more than a week ago, he'd instructed his business manager to contact Monteverde's creditors with guarantees.

Monteverde was effectively under Monterossan control.

Yet the victory felt hollow. He'd thought he would feel triumph, satisfaction. He'd thought he would feel Julianne's approval somehow. But all he felt was empty. As if he'd lost instead of won.

Antonella.

He didn't want to think about her, and yet he could think of nothing else. As the helicopter lifted off the pad and slid across the azure sky toward Monterosso, he thought he glimpsed her still sitting all alone on the terrace where he'd left her. Something twisted inside him, but he refused to examine it.

She was a beautiful, sensual, fascinating woman who was far more than he'd ever given her credit for. She was at turns stronger than anyone he knew, and more vulnerable than a child. She was both innocent and worldly. She set him on fire with a longing look, and tore him apart with her wounded indignation.

She loved him. And while he wanted to accept that love, wanted to turn around and take her with him back to Monterosso—where he wouldn't let her out of bed for a week at least—he couldn't do it. He'd accepted a woman's love once before, and it had ruined her.

Letting Antonella go was the hardest, kindest, most unselfish thing he'd ever done. He would not turn back now.

It was over.

CHAPTER FOURTEEN

THE summer was waning, the days growing shorter and the light growing longer as the sun tracked toward its winter home in the sky. Everything took on a golden hue in the late August afternoon. Antonella smiled at the little girl who jumped rope in the courtyard, her pigtails limned in warm light as they bounced with her movements.

"She is doing well," Signora Foretti, the director of the women's and children's shelter, said. "Her nightmares are less frequent now, and her therapist says she is making strides."

"I am very glad," Antonella replied. The little girl reminded her of herself in some ways. Shy, small, frightened of everyone and everything. She had been that way too, when she was that age.

"She looks forward to your visits, *Principessa*. She is always happy when you come to see her. As are all the souls who reside here."

Antonella swallowed a lump in her throat. "*Grazie, Signora*. I am honored to be here. If my experience helps just one woman to leave an abusive husband, or one child to know the abuse is not her fault, then I am pleased."

In the two months since she had returned home to

Monteverde, she had indeed done a few things differently. She still wished to attend university some day, but she'd been so busy since coming home that she'd had little time to do so. Instead, her days were spent at the shelter and in running her foundation.

She'd wanted to do something useful, and she'd found her purpose when she'd determined to visit the shelter. Dante supported her efforts, for which she was grateful. If he hadn't agreed to her sharing her experiences with others, or to her heading up an effort to help abused women and children, she wouldn't be able to do this. Because in sharing her experience, she also shared his. Not that she would dare to voice his story, but the fact she'd been abused by their father implied he had as well.

Rather than remaining a source of shame and anguish, her secret pain had become her strength. She couldn't save every woman and child, but she could work to save a good many of them.

Her foundation was growing in leaps and bounds; just this morning, her accountant had called and told her they'd had a very large foreign donation. She'd recently begun to think about taking the foundation's work international, and the money had come at exactly the right time. Surely it was a sign that she was meant to do this.

She said goodbye to Signora Foretti and her staff, then climbed into the waiting limo that would take her back to the palace. She would have rather driven her own car, but Signora Foretti had convinced her it was important for the occupants of the shelter to see her as the princess she was. It helped them to know that no one was exempt from abuse, not even the wealthy and privileged.

As always when she was alone, her thoughts turned to Cristiano. She'd heard nothing from him since the afternoon he'd left her on Lily's terrazzo and flown back to Monterosso. If Dante spoke with him at all, he did not mention it to her. Not that she'd told Dante of her affair with Cristiano, but perhaps her brother sensed that her emotions were tangled where it concerned the Monterossan Crown Prince.

Madonna mia, how long would it take to get over these feelings? Each day was as painful as the last, as long and lonely as the endless days since he'd left.

At least Monteverde was recovering, even if she wasn't. The ore was moving into the market at a good pace, and money was trickling into the economy from outside their borders. There had been a few setbacks, not the least of which was a bomb that had exploded in a crowded market two weeks ago. The market was less than a kilometer from the palace. Never before had they experienced the violence so close at hand.

Ten people had died in the attack. A Monterossan group claimed responsibility, though Cristiano's father was swift to issue a condemnation and to state the group had not acted with the approval or authority of the state.

Though there were Monteverdians who did not believe the King's statement, Antonella did. She believed because of Cristiano. He would be horrified by this turn of events, and he would have communicated that horror to his father. The blast would bring painful memories to the surface for him— memories he would not wish upon anyone. The bomb had been the work of extremists, not of mainstream Monterosso.

When they were almost at the palace, the car drew to a halt in a knot of traffic.

"What's going on?" Antonella asked the driver.

"I do not know, *Principessa,*" he replied. "Could be a protest."

Antonella took her mobile phone from her purse and dialed

Dante's private number. When he didn't answer, she called her sister-in-law.

"He didn't want to tell you," Isabel said. "But Prince Cristiano is here."

Antonella's heart felt like a lead weight in her chest. How long had Dante known that Cristiano would be here today? "Why would he not tell me, Isabel? Cristiano di Savaré is nothing to me. I have not spoken to him in months. It would be nice to say hello," she lied.

Isabel was silent. "Dante thinks mention of the prince causes you pain," she finally said. "He would have sent you away, but we had no notice of this visit until this morning."

This morning? *Madonna mia.* The bombing must have bothered Cristiano a great deal, until he could stay away no longer. Did he blame himself?

He must. It saddened her. How could he take so much onto himself? And how would she deal with seeing him again? What would she say? Did he miss her? Or was this simply a state visit?

So many possibilities swirled in her mind that she didn't know what to think or how to respond.

"I am stuck in traffic, so perhaps he will be gone again by the time I arrive," she said lightly.

Isabel sighed. "I think not, my dear. He is staying for dinner, and Dante has called several of his ministers to join us. Perhaps you should stay in a hotel for the night."

"Stay in a hotel?" As if she often checked into hotels while driving through town. As if she carried a suitcase with her for just such a purpose. "No, I'm coming home."

"Ella," Isabel said, "there is a woman."

"A woman?" she repeated dumbly.

A heavy sigh came through the phone. "Prince Cristiano is traveling with a companion."

* * *

Antonella looked at her reflection in the mirror with satisfaction. She wore an ice-blue gown that hugged her from breast to hip before falling in soft waves to the floor. The gown set off the grey of her eyes, which she'd taken care to line in dark kohl before smudging the color to replicate a just-got-out-of-bed look. A raspberry stain gave her lips that freshly kissed color she remembered so well.

Sad that it was only a memory, but she'd found no other man she wished to kiss.

She arranged her hair in a loose tumble of pinned curls that trailed down her back in a thick shiny mass. Once she slipped on her jewelry—an understated diamond pendant, teardrop earrings, and a small tiara—she took a deep breath for courage. She would get through this evening, and she would show Cristiano that she was over him completely.

She wasn't, of course, but he didn't have to know that. Obviously, he'd had no trouble moving on to another lover. The thought that he would bring the woman here, knowing he would most likely see her, his former lover, infuriated her.

She'd meant less than nothing to him. He was easily over her while she kept dwelling on every moment they'd spent together.

No more.

Antonella was purposely late to the cocktail hour. She'd considered skipping it altogether, but she wouldn't let Cristiano know he still had that kind of power over her. No, she decided that if she had to be there, she would make a grand entrance.

When she swept into the room, head held high, conversation ceased. All eyes turned to her. She was accustomed to such a reaction, had cultivated it in the past to her advantage, but now it made her feel self-conscious. She wanted to melt into the Persian carpet.

She knew where Cristiano stood the moment she walked

in, but she did not look at him. In her peripheral vision, she could make out a woman standing beside him. A lovely pale woman in glittering jewels and a mint silk dress.

"*Principessa*," a waiter said, stopping before her with a tray of champagne. She took a glass, more to have something to hold than because she wanted to drink it. The waiter moved away again, and conversation restarted. Isabel hurried over.

"You didn't have to come," she said.

"Don't be silly. Of course I had to."

"Oh, dear." Isabel bit her lip as she gazed over Antonella's shoulder.

"What's wrong?"

"Antonella."

She closed her eyes briefly as the deep, sexy voice reverberated through her. *Dear God, please give me strength.*

"Prince Cristiano," she replied, turning and smiling politely. "How lovely to see you again."

His eyes were as hot as ever. They scorched her as his gaze took her in from head to toe. "I wish to speak with you privately," he said, catching her off guard.

No small talk? No polite chit-chat?

He seemed so serious—and yet her inner voice sounded a warning. She could not be alone with this man ever again. Not if she wanted to maintain her dignity. "I'm sorry, Your Highness, but that is quite impossible. Dinner is about to be served."

He looked as if he would argue, but then he inclined his head in agreement. "After dinner, then."

"Yes, of course." She kept her smile in place and hoped he would go away. After dinner, she would find a reason to absent herself.

"May I escort you to the table?" he asked, reaching for her hand before giving her a chance to reply.

Heat blazed through her at the first touch of his skin against hers. She swallowed against the sudden dryness in her throat. "Certainly."

Thankfully, once she was seated, he moved away and took the seat that had been assigned to him.

Dinner was an interminable affair. Antonella didn't notice anything about what was served, or how it tasted. Cristiano sat a few places away, and though he spoke pleasantries with the people around him, she was aware of every move he made, as if he did it solely for her. Each time his fork touched his lips, she remembered his mouth on hers. Each time he sipped his wine, she pictured him in the dressing room, sipping wine with her and talking about his life.

His companion was a beautiful woman who smiled and laughed a lot. And no wonder. She was sharing the bed of a man who knew how to make a woman happy, at least physically. Antonella hated her—and she hated herself for feeling this way. It wasn't the woman's fault she'd captured Cristiano's attention, or that she was the current object of his desire.

As soon as the final course was served, Antonella placed her napkin on the table and excused herself, pleading a sudden headache. She just couldn't take another moment of pretending to be fine while the man she still loved—God help her—sat nearby with a new lover.

Cristiano's gaze bored into her as she stood. She forced herself to turn from those hot, seeking eyes and walk from the room.

The fastest way back to her rooms was across the courtyard. She hurried outside and down the broad stone steps, cursing as one spiked heel slipped between the cobblestones of the path that took her through the gardens.

"You should wear more sensible shoes."

Antonella wrenched her heel free and spun to find

Cristiano on the path behind her. Her breath caught. He was still as dark and devilish in his custom tuxedo as the first time she'd turned to find him standing outside her room on the yacht.

"What do you want?" she demanded. Anger was her only refuge. Anything less and she would crumple into an emotional mess. Perhaps when she was older, more jaded with her affairs, she would not feel everything so keenly. The thought did not give her comfort; it left her feeling hollow.

"I want to talk to you," he said.

"They make telephones for this purpose. You could have talked to me at any point in the past two months."

He took another step forward. His hands were shoved in his pockets. His expression, she noted, was less controlled than she'd thought. He seemed…uncertain.

"I missed you."

She wrapped her arms around herself. "Do not say such things," she bit out. "I don't want to hear it, Cristiano. I'm not falling into bed with you ever again, so please, *please* just go away and leave me alone."

He swore softly, raked a hand through his hair. "I can't go away. Not without you."

She put her hands over her ears, her heart thundering so hard that the movement was probably unnecessary. She could hear nothing but the pounding of her blood through her veins.

Cristiano gently grasped her wrists and pulled her hands away. "Listen to me."

"Let me go! You have no right—" She sucked in a breath to halt the sob that wanted to break free from the tightness in her chest. "You have no right, Cristiano. What would your girlfriend think?"

He blinked. "My girlfriend? What are you talking about?"

"The woman with you tonight," she practically shouted.

"You did not listen to a thing we talked about at the table, did you?" he said, looking suddenly amused. But he let her go.

She took a step back. "I have a headache," she lied. "I was preoccupied."

"Rosina is my third cousin on my mother's side. She is a doctor, and head of a surgical program that works with traumatic injuries. Bomb blasts, *tesoro mio*. I have brought her to Monteverde so she can offer her expertise."

His cousin? A doctor? Heat crept across her skin. She'd heard nothing of the conversation, it was true. Her mind had been racing with thoughts of him. She'd withdrawn into herself in order to insulate her heart. She couldn't even remember what she'd talked about with the matron seated beside her.

"That is good of you," she heard herself say. Inane response.

"The bombing is my fault. It is the least I can do."

She stifled a defeated sigh. *Oh, Cristiano.* "How is it your fault? You would never sanction such a thing."

He shook his head. "No, of course not. But you warned me I had not considered how deep resentments went, that I could not single-handedly end this war of ideology between our nations. You were right."

"Monteverde is recovering, thanks to you. You saved us from ruin. And you can't prevent a few extremists from trying to take us all backwards. The bombing is not your fault."

His gaze dropped for a moment. "Perhaps you are right. Perhaps I take too much upon myself." When he lifted his head, what she saw in his eyes made her blood beat. "I dragged you beneath our control without regard to what was best for Monteverdians. I have come to change that."

"I don't understand."

"We can only move forward if we work together, not if one nation dictates terms to another. Dante is a good man. He is a good King, and he is the right person to guide this nation. Our governments will work side by side to end the mistrust and hostility."

She gazed at him in wonder. "You have returned the mineral rights?"

"*Si*. We are guarantors of your debt, not your overlords."

"But Dante could sell the ore to someone other than Vega." And they could use the money to do what they wished, not what Monterosso wanted them to do. It was a huge concession on his part—and it was contrary to everything he'd ever wanted.

Cristiano shrugged, though she knew he did not do so lightly. "Then Raúl must either pay a good price or see the ore go to his competitors. I assure you he will not allow that to happen."

"Why are you doing this?"

His expression was haggard for a moment. "I mistakenly thought that Monterossans were superior, that it was simply Monteverdian greed and recalcitrance that was prolonging the hostility between us. I thought if I could control Monteverde, I could end it. I was wrong."

"I'm so sorry, Cristiano."

"What do you have to be sorry for? You tried to tell me."

She swallowed. "I'm just sorry that it hasn't given you the peace you wanted. The personal peace, I mean."

"Ah, yes. Julianne's ghost." He tilted his head back for a moment, then speared her with an intense look. "I have made many mistakes she would not have wanted me to make. But she is gone now and I am finally ready to move on with my life. She knew what she was doing when she went on that aid mission. It was what she was trained to do. If I'd stopped her then, I wouldn't have been able to stop her the next time"

She gave him a watery smile. He'd finally accepted that it wasn't his fault. He was ready to live again. It was what she wanted for him, all she'd ever wanted. "I'm happy for you, Cristiano. And I hope you will be happy, that you will find someone—"

"I have found someone," he said softly. "I have found you."

Her knees were so weak she had to put her hand against the stone balustrade to steady herself. "Please don't torment me, Cristiano. I can't bear to watch you walk away again."

He crossed the distance between them, lifted his hand to her cheek. His fingers shook. But for that, she would have turned away. That one movement, that single vulnerability, made her think he might feel something for her after all.

"It is hard for me," he said. "Hard to let go, to feel love when it terrifies me that I could lose you too. But I do. I love you, Antonella."

She couldn't stop the tear that spilled down her cheek. "I want to believe you. But I am afraid."

He pulled her into his embrace, spanning the back of her head with one broad hand and cradling her to his chest as if she were precious to him. "No, you are the bravest person I know. Braver than I."

"No—"

"Yes. I thought bravery was found in things like saving princesses from falling trees, but it goes far deeper. True bravery comes from facing the demons of your past, from refusing to back down from the hard truths. You taught me that. It has taken me too long to realize the truth, but I wish to spend my days making it up to you."

She couldn't stop her arms from going around him, from holding him tight. Because if this weren't true, if it were all a dream, she still wanted to remember the hard feel of him against her body one last time.

Before she could speak, he tilted her head back and kissed her. The kiss was everything she remembered—and more.

"Tell me you still love me, Antonella," he whispered against her cheek. His mouth trailed over her jaw, down her neck. "Tell me I haven't ruined your feelings for me."

Every nerve ending in her body zinged with heat and need. And yet she was still afraid.

"I—I need time," she said.

He lifted his head, disappointment evident in his expression. "Of course. This is too much, too soon. But I have never been good at patience when I know what I want. For you, I will try."

"What *do* you want, Cristiano?"

He seemed surprised. "You. I want you. I thought I said this."

She lowered her lashes, studied the crisp white pleats of his shirt. Her pulse was out of control, and yet she needed to be certain of his meaning. "But I don't know what that means, exactly. You might wish to carry on a grand affair or—"

"Antonella, *amore mio*," he interrupted, cupping her face in his hands and tilting her head back. "Yes, I want a grand affair. I want one that lasts a lifetime. I want you by my side every day. I want you to be my princess, my queen, and the mother of my children."

Her breath caught. "You are certain of this? It will not be easy for you. I am Monteverdian, and—"

"I love you, Antonella. I won't make excuses for it, and I won't compromise. If I had to renounce my place in the succession for you, I would do so."

"I would never ask that of you," she vowed.

He kissed her forehead. "You would have no choice. To be with you, I would give up far more than a throne."

"But I don't want you to give up anything."

He smiled, and the hint of vulnerability in it twisted her heart. "Then tell me you will marry me and put me out of my misery. Because I've given up sleep for the last two months. I've also given up happiness. If you marry me, I will get these things back."

Her heart was swelling, daring to believe—

"I hope you are certain of this."

"More certain than I've ever been."

She closed her eyes, breathing in the scent of him. He was home to her. Home, life, love—everything she'd ever wanted. "I believe in you, Cristiano. I trust you with my soul. I have almost from the first moment I met you."

"Does this mean you love me? That you will marry me?"

Leap, Antonella. Let him catch you. "I do. And I will."

"*Grazie a Dio,*" he breathed. "*Non posso vivere senza voi.*"

"I can't live without you either, Cristiano. *Ti amo.*"

EPILOGUE

ANTONELLA DI SAVARÉ, Her Royal Highness the Crown Princess of Monterosso, lounged in a chair by the pool, her eyes closed as the warm sun beat down on her skin. It felt so good, especially since she'd gotten little sleep the night before.

She could hear the high-pitched laughter, the splashing, but she knew Signora Giovanni had everything under control.

A shadow fell over her. She didn't need to open her eyes to know who it was. She would know his scent anywhere. And even if she couldn't smell a thing, she would still know it was him. Her husband gave off an electric vibe that crackled through her body each time he was near.

She kept her eyes closed, but she couldn't stop the smile that tugged at the corners of her lips.

"I know you are awake," he said, dropping to her side. A kiss landed on her forehead.

Antonella pouted. "Kiss me properly, Cristiano."

"Look at me."

She obeyed and he kissed her so thoroughly that she was panting when he pulled away.

"I want you," he growled. "Now."

Antonella stretched like a cat. "You did not have enough of me last night?"

"You know I did not. Antonio needed you when things were just getting interesting."

She yawned. "He is a demanding baby."

Cristiano's fingers ghosted over her skin, over the smoothness of her belly. She'd worked hard to get her shape back again, though Cristiano had insisted she was beautiful to him whether she carried an extra few pounds or not.

"You are tired," he said. "Go inside and sleep. I will tell Signora Giovanni where you have gone."

"I promised Cristiana I would take her to get *gelato* later."

"We have ice cream here," he said in disbelief.

"I know, but your daughter likes to go to the shop and order for herself."

"She is two. How is this possible?"

Antonella shrugged. "It just is. I believe her Uncle Dante taught her."

Cristiano shook his head. "Very well, but I will take her. You must rest. Between the children and your work with the foundation, I am worried you stretch yourself thin."

"I am fine, Cristiano." She ran her fingers along his arm. She loved touching him. And the more she touched him, the less she wanted to sleep. "How did your meeting go today?"

"Very well. Dante and Isabel send their love, by the way. They wish us to join them tomorrow for dinner."

Antonella smiled. In the three years since she'd married Cristiano, life had been very good. They had two beautiful children, their nations were at peace, and prosperity had once again returned to Monteverde. There were still checkpoints on the border, and factions that required surveillance, but there'd been no violence of any kind in more than a year now. They'd even had an increase in the number of marriage license applications between the two nations.

"I look forward to it," she said. "But I look forward to something else even more."

His eyes blazed. "You need sleep, *amore mio*. Do not tempt me."

She let her hand settle on the bulge of his erection. "You want me."

"Oh, yes, I want you."

"I will sleep better if you make love to me first."

He scooped her into his arms, then called out to Signora Giovanni. Antonella laughed as he carried her toward their bedroom. "You are so easy to seduce."

He kicked the bedroom door shut behind him, locked it. "I seem to remember that I tried to refuse you the first time we made love, but you would not let me."

"Believe me," Antonella said as he set her down and stripped her out of her bathing suit, "I am profoundly grateful you were not so strong-willed as you pretended."

He looked at her with mock offense. "Not strong-willed? I am about to show you how determined I can be."

"And what are you determined to do, my love?"

"I am determined to prove to you that you complete me. Without you, I would still be lost."

Her eyes filled with tears. "I love you, Cristiano."

He took her in his arms and kissed her. "And *that* is what I am profoundly grateful for."

Coming Next Month

in **Harlequin Presents® EXTRA.** Available June 8, 2010.

Coming Next Month

in **Harlequin Presents®.** Available June 29, 2010.

LARGER-PRINT
BOOKS!

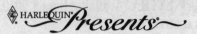

GET 2 FREE LARGER-PRINT
NOVELS PLUS 2 FREE GIFTS!

YES! Please send me 2 FREE LARGER-PRINT Harlequin Presents® novels and my 2 FREE gifts (gifts are worth about $10). After receiving them, if I don't wish to receive any more books, I can return the shipping statement marked "cancel". If I don't cancel, I will receive 6 brand-new novels every month and be billed just $4.55 per book in the U.S. or $5.24 per book in Canada. That's a saving of at least 13% off the cover price! It's quite a bargain! Shipping and handling is just 50¢ per book.* I understand that accepting the 2 free books and gifts places me under no obligation to buy anything. I can always return a shipment and cancel at any time. Even if I never buy another book, the two free books and gifts are mine to keep forever.

176/376 HDN E5NG

Name _____ (PLEASE PRINT) _____

Address _____ Apt. # _____

City _____ State/Prov. _____ Zip/Postal Code _____

Signature (if under 18, a parent or guardian must sign) _____

Mail to the **Harlequin Reader Service:**
IN U.S.A.: P.O. Box 1867, Buffalo, NY 14240-1867
IN CANADA: P.O. Box 609, Fort Erie, Ontario L2A 5X3

Not valid for current subscribers to Harlequin Presents Larger-Print books.

**Are you a subscriber to Harlequin Presents books
and want to receive the larger-print edition?
Call 1-800-873-8635 today!**

* Terms and prices subject to change without notice. Prices do not include applicable taxes. Sales tax applicable in N.Y. Canadian residents will be charged applicable provincial taxes and GST. Offer not valid in Quebec. This offer is limited to one order per household. All orders subject to approval. Credit or debit balances in a customer's account(s) may be offset by any other outstanding balance owed by or to the customer. Please allow 4 to 6 weeks for delivery. Offer available while quantities last.

Your Privacy: Harlequin Books is committed to protecting your privacy. Our Privacy Policy is available online at www.eHarlequin.com or upon request from the Reader Service. From time to time we make our lists of customers available to reputable third parties who may have a product or service of interest to you. If you would prefer we not share your name and address, please check here. ☐

Help us get it right—We strive for accurate, respectful and relevant communications. To clarify or modify your communication preferences, visit us at www.ReaderService.com/consumerschoice.

HPLP10R

HARLEQUIN®

A Romance

FOR EVERY MOOD™

Spotlight on
Heart & Home

Heartwarming romances
where love can happen
right when you least expect it.

See the next page to enjoy a sneak peek
from Silhouette Special Edition®,
a Heart and Home series.

*Introducing McFARLANE'S PERFECT BRIDE
by USA TODAY bestselling author Christine Rimmer,
from Silhouette Special Edition®.*

Entranced. Captivated. Enchanted.

Connor sat across the table from Tori Jones and couldn't help thinking that those words exactly described what effect the small-town schoolteacher had on him. He might as well stop trying to tell himself he wasn't interested. He was powerfully drawn to her.

Clearly, he should have dated more when he was younger.

There had been a couple of other women since Jennifer had walked out on him. But he had never been entranced. Or captivated. Or enchanted.

Until now.

He wanted her—*her*, Tori Jones, in particular. Not just someone suitably attractive and well-bred, as Jennifer had been. Not just someone sophisticated, sexually exciting and discreet, which pretty much described the two women he'd dated after his marriage crashed and burned.

It came to him that he...he *liked* this woman. And that was new to him. He liked her quick wit, her wisdom and her big heart. He liked the passion in her voice when she talked about things she believed in.

He liked *her*. And suddenly it mattered all out of proportion that she might like him, too.

Was he losing it? He couldn't help but wonder. Was he cracking under the strain—of the soured economy, the McFarlane House setbacks, his divorce, the scary changes in his son? Of the changes he'd decided he needed to make in his life and himself?

Strangely, right then, on his first date with Tori Jones, he didn't care if he just might be going over the edge. He was having a great time—having *fun*, of all things—and he didn't want it to end.

Is Connor finally able to admit his feelings to Tori, and are they reciprocated?
Find out in MCFARLANE'S PERFECT BRIDE
by USA TODAY bestselling author Christine Rimmer.
Available July 2010,
only from Silhouette Special Edition®.

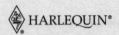

Showcase

LESLIE KELLY
Naturally Naughty

Wicked & Willing

On sale June 8

Reader favorites from the most talented voices in romance

Save $1.00 on the purchase of 1 or more Harlequin® Showcase books.

SAVE $1.00 on the purchase of 1 or more Harlequin® Showcase books.

Coupon expires November 30, 2010. Redeemable at participating retail outlets.
Limit one coupon per customer. Valid in the U.S.A. and Canada only.

52609057

Canadian Retailers: Harlequin Enterprises Limited will pay the face value of this coupon plus 10.25¢ if submitted by customer for this product only. Any other use constitutes fraud. Coupon is nonassignable. Void if taxed, prohibited or restricted by law. Consumer must pay any government taxes. Void if copied. Nielsen Clearing House ("NCH") customers submit coupons and proof of sales to Harlequin Enterprises Limited, P.O. Box 3000, Saint John, NB E2L 4L3, Canada. Non-NCH retailer—for reimbursement submit coupons and proof of sales directly to Harlequin Enterprises Limited, Retail Marketing Department, 225 Duncan Mill Rd., Don Mills, ON M3B 3K9, Canada.

U.S. Retailers: Harlequin Enterprises Limited will pay the face value of this coupon plus 8¢ if submitted by customer for this product only. Any other use constitutes fraud. Coupon is nonassignable. Void if taxed, prohibited or restricted by law. Consumer must pay any government taxes. Void if copied. For reimbursement submit coupons and proof of sales directly to Harlequin Enterprises Limited, P.O. Box 880478, El Paso, TX 88588-0478, U.S.A. Cash value 1/100 cents.

5 65373 00076 2   (8100)0 11654

® and TM are trademarks owned and used by the trademark owner and/or its licensee.
© 2010 Harlequin Enterprises Limited

HSCCOUP0610